THE ABYSS

JC RYAN

By JC Ryan

Dedicated to my good friend Mitch Pender, a military dog trainer, for giving me the idea for this series and guiding me through the intricate and amazing capabilities and psychology of those majestic four-legged soldiers.

Mitch has a lifetime of experience and an exceptional depth of knowledge as a military dog handler and trainer.

I am deeply indebted to my friend, co-author, co-conspirator, and mentor, David Lee, who, with his in-depth understanding of Hong Kong and China, came up with the idea for this novel and tirelessly assisted me in developing the outline and advised and supported me throughout the entire writing process.

Vinci Books

vinci-books.com

Published by Vinci Books Ltd in 2025

1

A CIP catalogue record for this book is available from the British Library.
Paperback ISBN: 9781036704780

Major characters

Rex Dalton: Former black operations specialist working for CRC.

Catia: Married to Rex. Former Mossad mission support specialist.

Digger: A black Dutch Shepherd. Former military dog. Rex and Catia's companion.

Josh Farley: Black operations specialist working for CRC. Friend of Rex, Catia, and Digger.

Marissa: Married to Josh. Black operations specialist working for CRC. Friend of Rex, Catia, and Digger.

John Brandt: CEO of CRC (Crisis Response Consultancy), a private military contractor specializing in black operations on behalf of their clients such as the CIA and other US security agencies.

Christelle Brandt née Proll: former deputy director of the DGSE, the French equivalent of the American CIA. Married to John Brandt.

Greg Wade: Team leader of CRC's small but highly skilled group of IT specialists.

Rehka Gyan: IT expert. Greg's love interest.

Howard Lawrence: Director of the CIA.

Martin Richardson: Deputy director in charge of CIA operations.

Ollie Campbell: A CIA field agent during the Cold War and friend of John Brandt.

Sean Woods: Operation Peregrine IT team lead.

Lydia Andrews: Liaison between the FBI and Operation Peregrine.

Stacie Barrett: Operation Peregrine analyst team lead.

Jordyn Lancaster: Codename Stardust. The senior senator from New York, chairperson of the Senate Committee on Foreign Relations.

Sun Yan: Codename Flat Arrow. Computer expert, formerly working for Unit 61398, part of the Information Operations and Information Warfare, the cyberwarfare division of the People's Liberation Army (PLA). Defected to the USA.

General Lang Jianhong: Codename Deep Mantis. Commander of the People's Liberation Army (PLA) Ground Force.

General Dai Min: a senior general in the PLA (People's Liberation Army) in charge of China's nuclear arsenal.

General Jin Ping: in charge of Information Operations and Information Warfare, the cyber warfare division of the PLA.

Li Lingxin: Former President of the PRC (People's Republic of China).

Liao Qigang: Current President of the PRC (People's Republic of China).

Tao Huan: Chairman of the Central Military Commission, the head of the military.

Mao Xinya: Minister of Agriculture and Rural Affairs.

ROC: Republic of China, more commonly referred to as Taiwan.

PRC: People's Republic of China, commonly referred to as China.

PLA: People's Liberation Army.

CCP: Chinese Communist Party.

CWC: Cold War Council, a fictitious group chaired by the President of the United States.

About The Abyss

The Abyss is the sequel to Holes In The Wall.

The US intelligence agencies are dusting off their play-books from the first Cold War as they find themselves in a new Cold War, this time with China.

The Operation Peregrine team is aware that China has plans for the invasion of Taiwan, but they also realize they have a severe lack of intelligence from inside the PRC. So, they launch an initiative to recruit a high-ranking general in the People's Liberation Army to spy for them.

But then it is discovered that China is facing a famine much worse than the Great Chinese Famine of 1959 to 1961, during which thirty million starved to death.

A hellish abyss of food insecurity and starvation—the perfect breeding ground for war.

Prologue

Zhongnanhai, Beijing, China

Ever since taking office, President Liao Qigang's sleeping habits had become erratic. Stress had been his ever-present companion, stalking him every waking moment, and nightmares haunted his dreams. On a good night, he'd get six hours of sleep, but those were few and far between. Most nights, he would get four to five hours, and then there were the nights when he got no sleep at all—like tonight. The prospect of invading Taiwan and the international repercussions, including the likelihood of war with America and its allies, weighed heavily on him as he waited for the call from General Xia, who was in charge of the operation.

And if the threat of war was not enough to keep Liao in a constant state of despondency, the reports about severe flooding in the Kwei Zhou area in the southwestern part of the country were making a generous contribution to his acute dyspepsia.

The benefit of state-controlled media is that the state

determines what information is released to the public. The flood was labeled as 'lots of rain.' The number of people displaced was quoted as half a million, while the actual number was about three times that. The number of dead, which was actually more than 100,000, was reported to be 40,000.

Even so, the president couldn't dare to visit the stricken area because that would make it look as if there really had been a major disaster.

Though that kind of disingenuous reporting helped keep the populace's stress and anxiety levels down, it did nothing for the president's.

Liao felt the knot in his stomach as he looked at the information about the threatening disaster posed by the overflowing of the Three Gorges Dam. The City of Wuhan had already been flooded. Two major lakes on both sides of the Yangtze River functioned as natural draining reservoirs for excessive water flowing down the river. The Por Yang Hu Lake on the northern side of the Yangtze, normally about 3,000 square miles, had in three days grown to more than 4,000 square miles. If the Three Gorges Dam gave way, 450 million, one-third of China's total population, would be negatively impacted, and as many as 45 million people would either die or suffer from severe health issues.

He took a long deep breath and let it out slowly and noisily.

At the break of dawn, with no call from Xia and no breaking news out of Taiwan on any of the news channels, he knew the operation must've run into some kind of problem.

He felt relief washing over him. China would not be going to war today. "But there are things worse than war— famine. I can only hope that we will never fall over that cliff

2

into the hellish abyss of food insecurity and starvation," he mumbled softly.

He took a hot shower and put on a clean suit, then ordered his favorite breakfast of congee (rice porridge), pancakes with eggs, and a pot of tea.

By 8:00 a.m., when Mao Xinya, the Minister of Agriculture and Rural Affairs, entered his office, Liao felt almost rejuvenated.

It was with no small measure of trepidation that Mao Xinya arrived at Zhongnanhai. Messengers bearing bad news were not usually at peril for merely conveying the message. But Mao Xinya was no ordinary messenger; he was the Minister of Agriculture and Rural Affairs, a position he had held for more than a decade.

In the world's fourth-largest and most populous country, his responsibilities were vast: agriculture and environmental issues relating to agriculture, fishery, consumer affairs, animal husbandry, horticulture, animal welfare, foodstuffs, hunting and game management, as well as higher education and research in the field of agricultural sciences.

To be concise, Mao Xinya carried the ultimate responsibility for the production of the food that the 1.4 billion citizens of China put on their tables every day.

For almost four weeks, Mao and his advisors worked meticulously and slept very little to collect and verify data, analyzed same, made projections, and wrote their conclusions down in a report—the fount of Mao's disquiet—currently in his briefcase.

During the Great Chinese Famine of 1959 to 1961, thirty million had starved to death. In addition, miscarriages due to malnutrition and abortions because there was no food for babies, claimed another thirty million.

Mao was about to tell the President that the country was facing another famine—this one would make the Great Famine pale in comparison.

Bringing Professor Lei Hai, senior agronomist and grain specialist, to answer the technical questions he was bound to be asked provided little comfort.

Whether the fact that he was distantly related to the great Chairman Mao Tse-tung would count in his favor, he would know shortly.

Chapter One

FIRST DAY ON THE JOB

CIA Headquarters, Langley, Virginia, USA

It was Monday morning shortly before eight when John pulled up in his designated parking space at Langley. He switched the engine off and looked at his wife, Christelle. "This is it, your first day on the job. Excited?"

She smiled and nodded. "Just like old times." Christelle was a tall woman with an athletic build, green eyes, and blond hair that didn't come out of a bottle—she was a head-turner. She was formally dressed in a charcoal pantsuit. Attentiveness and intelligence radiated from her persona.

John chuckled. "Yep, except now we're up against the Chinese communists instead of the Russians, we're forty years older, and we have a service dog to watch over us."

Said service dog was in the backseat. Her name was Cupcake, a seven-month-old, short-haired, brindle-colored Dutch Shepherd. She was a gift to them from Rex and

Catia when John got out of the hospital after brain surgery five months ago.

"I don't feel forty years older. I barely feel forty."

"And you don't look a day older," said John with a big smile.

"Flattery will get you everywhere, my dear."

John stood at six-foot-two in his socks. A handsome man with gray hair and hazel eyes, stately comportment, and in excellent shape for someone of seventy-four years.

Christelle, a former deputy director of the DGSE, the French equivalent of the American CIA, had worked with John on a few joint missions in their younger days during the Cold War. There was a romantic spark between them back then, but the Atlantic Ocean and work had put an end to it. More than thirty years after their last joint mission, they caught up again. The old flame was rekindled, and two months after Christelle's retirement, she and John were married.

They had plans to settle on the Ranch, a 20,000-acre property in Yavapai County, in the western part of Arizona, CRC'S headquarters and training facility. However, they had to change their plans when they were on their way back to the Ranch after their honeymoon in Vietnam. Richardson contacted Brandt and asked him to divert the flight and come to Langley to discuss a very urgent matter. The pressing issue was the Operation Middle Kingdom Plan.

Since then, John and Christelle had been living in an apartment fifteen minutes' drive from CIA headquarters.

It had been nearly three months since the defection of Flat Arrow, the codename for a senior computer programmer working for China's foremost military hacking outfit, Unit 61398, a subdivision of the Information Operations and Information Warfare division, the cyberwarfare arm of the People's Liberation Army (PLA).

The insider knowledge about Unit 61398's activities brought over by Flat Arrow was a significant haul for the US intelligence community. It helped them to identify and rectify the vulnerabilities in their own computer networks, and it enabled them to exploit the vulnerabilities in the PRC's networks.

But it was the details of Operation Middle Kingdom, delivered by Flat Arrow, that shook the foundations of the US intelligence community.

Soon dubbed the MK Plan, it was the blueprint conceived by a top-secret power group, who called themselves the Trustees, which included the Chinese President and ten senior generals from the People's Liberation Army (PLA) to dethrone America as the world's only superpower and achieve Mao Tse-tung's hundred-year plan—the entire world under Chinese communist rule by 2049—twenty-five years ahead of time.

There was no ambiguity in the MK Plan—China was on the verge of instigating a series of actions that would bring them into direct conflict with most of their neighbors and the USA. It was equally clear that unless China was dissuaded from its chosen course, a world war was inevitable.

Within days of receiving the MK Plan, the CIA had obtained presidential authorization to launch Operation Peregrine, a Cold War-like strategy aimed at containing China's expansionist ideals and prevent an all-out war, which would, without doubt, see the use of nuclear weapons.

After reading the MK Plan, Martin Richardson, the deputy director in charge of CIA operations, persuaded

John Brandt to take control of Operation Peregrine. John was a veteran of the Cold War who left the CIA in 1995. Six years later, in 2001, after the 9/11 attacks, he had established CRC (Crisis Response Consultancy), a private military contractor specializing in black operations on behalf of the CIA and other US security agencies.

Christelle opened the rear passenger door for Cupcake, took her leash, and hooked her arm into her husband's as they approached the front entrance of the George Bush Center for Intelligence colloquially known as the CIA Headquarters.

For the past three months, since John took charge of Operation Peregrine, despite being newlyweds, Christelle hadn't seen much of him. She and Cupcake had visited every noteworthy, and some not so noteworthy, statue, museum, and historical and contemporary building in the Langley and D.C. areas, including the White House and the Capitol Building.

After a lifetime in the spy business, she knew what was at stake, and intelligence officers seldom had the luxury of nine-to-five shifts. She supported and encouraged John, and she never complained, but that didn't prevent her from getting bored and a little frustrated with her dreary daily routine and lack of intellectual stimulation.

John took notice and had been thinking about a solution when he got home one night and found her working on a large petit point tapestry. She might as well have said, "John, I've had enough of museums and statues and art galleries." The next morning John spoke to Richardson.

Richardson took the matter to Howard Lawrence, the director of the CIA. Lawrence thought it was a matter for the Commander in Chief to decide. Therefore, he went to see the president, whose response was, "Bloody hell. You've got a senior Cold War veteran, a former deputy director of the DGSE, no less, sitting around idle, making tapestries, and keeping a dog company?"

"I'm afraid so, sir. I'd like her to join the Peregrine team, but we don't have any precedents for it."

"Well, if I understand you correctly, she's been working on joint missions with us since the Cold War and on another handful of missions over the past few years. And she knows as much about Peregrine as her husband knows. In other words, there's no trust issue?"

"None at all, sir."

"So, what's the holdup? Put her to work already. And if your French counterpart has any issues, let me know, I'll give their president a call. I presume the French hate the idea of a Chinese flag flying over France just as much as we hate the idea of it flying over America."

It was Friday afternoon, and John went home early to take his lovely wife out for dinner.

At the restaurant that evening, after placing their orders, it didn't take long before Christelle said, "John, you've got something on your mind. I'd like to hear it."

He managed to keep an impassive composure. "Well, I've got a vacancy on the Peregrine team, and I'm at a loss as to whom I should recruit."

"What's the job description?"

"I need someone with Cold War experience."

"Okay, but what specialty?"

"Strategic thinking, planning, managing agents and such—"

"And you don't know anyone like that?"

John shook his head. "The thing is, it must be a woman; she must be over sixty-five, and she must be very beautiful—"

Christelle leaned forward, "What's—"

John interjected, "Oh, and she must also be French and the former deputy director of the DGSE—"

"John!" Christelle had the most beautiful smile. "How did you pull that off?"

"Howard Lawrence got the president's permission—"

"You mean the President of the United States?"

"Uh-huh."

"But what about the DGSE? My terms of employment stated that I can't work for another country's intelligence service without explicit permission from the director—"

John held his hand up. "Don't worry, Lawrence called him. He says it was an easy sell once he gave your former boss a summary overview of the MK Plan. He agreed on the proviso that we share information pertaining to France with them."

"When do I start?"

"Monday morning."

"We'll have to get someone to take care of Cupcake while we're at work—"

John chuckled. "She's part of the deal. Her job description is to provide aid and comfort to you and me and anyone else on the team who might need it."

Christelle's face was beaming, and her eyes were sparkling.

And twelve time zones away, the Chinese intelligence agencies were totally unaware of the formidable former spymaster who had joined the ranks of their adversaries.

Chapter Two

HUMAN ASSETS AND DISINFORMATION

CIA Headquarters, Langley, Virginia, USA

The security guards at the entry to the Operation Peregrine command center were frowning when they let the second couple with a dog through the security gates but didn't make any comments until the visitors were out of earshot. The latest couple was much younger than the previous, but their big black Dutch Shepherd was much older than the previous dog. The guards had no need to know what Operation Peregrine was about, but it didn't stop them from wondering if the place had gone to the dogs or why, all of a sudden, the operation required service dogs or what role dogs could play in a spook operation.

A few minutes before 10:00 a.m., Director Howard Lawrence and Deputy Director Martin Richardson also passed through their security checkpoint and entered the Peregrine command center.

In the meeting room, Lawrence and Richardson found John, Christelle, Rex, Catia, Ollie Campbell, and of course,

Digger and Cupcake. Ollie was a former CIA field agent during the Cold War and a friend of John Brandt, whom he had called back into service to work on Operation Peregrine.

As usual, when Digger saw everyone shaking hands, he sat down next to Rex and extended his right paw for a shake. Cupcake was a quick study; she sat down next to Digger and followed his example to the delight of Lawrence and Richardson, who had never met any of them 'in-person.'

Although it was Catia's first visit to CIA headquarters, she had met everyone around the table on prior occasions. Her situation was similar to Christelle's in that she had worked for Mossad, the Israeli intelligence agency. However, since she and Rex got married a few years ago, she had been granted freelance status. That meant she could work for both CRC and Mossad as and when required if there were no conflicts of interest.

Digger and Cupcake retreated, each to their own corner, to chew on their kongs filled with beef jerky when the meeting started. The kong was an oddly-shaped toy, part cylinder, part cone, with indentations that made it look like a hard-plastic snowman. A hole runs through it from top to bottom, which could be stuffed with delicacies such as jerky, peanut butter, and other treats. It was always a joy to see the dogs' absolute ecstasy when they saw their kongs.

The purpose of the meeting was to inform Lawrence about the team's progress and plans for the future so that he could prepare his brief for the president and his secret Cold War Council (CWC) the next day.

The first half-hour was taken up by a retrospective of Peregrine's activities and achievements since its inception three months ago.

Several agents of China's MSS (Ministry of State Security) had been arrested over the past three months, and they had provided a treasure trove of information to the FBI's counterintelligence officers. As a result of this information, across the country, many prominent people, which included state and federal politicians, judges, mayors, government officials, and such, had come to the attention of the FBI's counterintelligence division. Some were bribed by the MSS, some blackmailed. Others hated capitalism. Some didn't even know they were informants for a hostile regime. As a result, some of them received visits from the FBI, were arrested, and charged with espionage. Some received visits and received defensive briefings. And some received no visits; they were watched very closely.

Most noteworthy among those who received defensive briefings was Senator Lancaster, the senior senator from New York. She was furious when she learned that the MSS had been actively setting her up for extortion. It didn't take much to persuade her to work closely with the FBI members of the Peregrine team to turn the tables on the MSS.

With the information provided by Flat Arrow and the efforts of the Peregrine IT team, significant inroads had been made into the PRC's military and intelligence computer networks, which produced much-needed intelligence about their plans and activities.

And last but not least, a week ago, Rex and his team of special operators had foiled the PRC's attempt to take control of the Strait of Malacca and, consequently, the South China Sea.

"Your team has produced spectacular results in a very short time, John," said Lawrence.

"Thank you, Howard, but impressive as it might seem, we've only been playing catchup. We're still a long way behind. The catchup effort must continue and expand in scope and effort, but we should launch new initiatives to put us on the front foot."

"What do you have in mind?"

John deferred to Ollie to explain.

Ollie lost both his legs in a shooting incident in Dresden, East Germany, during the Cold War. John was with him when it happened and helped him out of Dresden across the border into West Germany and safety. After Ollie had recovered from the wounds but wheelchair-bound for life, he returned to a desk job at the agency. What Ollie Campbell had lost in mobility, he more than made up with his intellect. And ever since, until the Berlin Wall finally came down, the Stasi and KGB had been regretting the day they'd shot Ollie Campbell. The man with no legs, from 4800 miles away, kept their best agents and spymasters running in circles while they were consuming inordinate amounts of antacid and headache tablets.

Ollie held up two fingers. "One, recruitment of human assets inside China. Two, disinformation."

"I'm listening," said Lawrence.

They spent another hour discussing the details. The plan was ambitious and daring and, if successful, would cause havoc among the authors of the MK Plan and in the ranks of the MSS.

Lawrence approved of the plan and undertook to inform the CWC the next day. Then he brought up another topic. "I think the time has come to inform some of our allies about the MK Plan. What do you think?" The question was directed at everyone in the room.

"We've been discussing that for the past few days and this morning before you and Martin arrived," said John. "Our concern is security; the more people who know about the MK Plan, the greater the chance that it might reach the ears of the Chinese. Even so, we know it is wishful thinking to expect the Chinese will forever remain unaware of what we have. Hence, for as long as they're unsuspecting, we should make every effort to build our own network of human intelligence assets as quickly as possible. And we could use all the help we can get from our friends."

"Makes sense," said Lawrence. "What do you have in mind?"

"What we suggest is that we inform only the heads of intelligence of the countries that need to know and can help us establish our spy network in China."

"Such as?"

"The British, because they've maintained assets in the region after returning Hong Kong to China in 1997. We suggest that Martin goes over to London to brief the head of the Firm."

Lawrence and Richardson agreed.

There is a very close and amicable working relationship between the British Secret Intelligence Service (SIS), commonly known as MI6, and the CIA. The MI6 people called their counterparts in the CIA 'the Cousins' and the CIA 'the Company'; the Americans called them 'the Friends' and MI6 'the Firm.'

"The French," John was smiling, "not only because their charming former deputy director is now on our payroll, but also because of their influence in Vietnam, a former colony and neighbor of China. There are an estimated two million ethnic Chinese living in Vietnam. Many of them travel to China to visit family or do business there. It's fertile hunting grounds for the recruitment of informants. We suggest that said charming former deputy director goes over to Paris to brief her former boss."

Rex and Catia were smiling. Clearly, married life was according well with John.

"And Israel," continued John. "I'll let Rex explain what we have in mind. It's his idea."

"Well, General Lang is the guy who lost the MK Plan," Rex started. "I'm convinced the rest of the Trustees don't know; otherwise, Lang would not be around anymore, and they would've changed the plan. But sooner or later, they'll realize that their plan has been leaked if we keep sabotaging their operations. I'm not sure how they'll figure out it was Lang who lost the plan, but it will be the end of the commander of China's ground forces when they do. No one knows that better than Lang himself. I think he's a very worried man. He should be our first target.

"The next targets, Generals Dai Min and Wan Huang, who were actively involved in the defection of General Yuan Lee last year, are in the same boat as Lang. Though they haven't lost top-secret information, they probably didn't tell their co-trustees how they collaborated with the CIA to help General Yuan Lee escape from China. And that might not sit very well with the other Trustees."

"Good. But how would you go about recruiting them?" asked Lawrence.

"With the help of the Israelis, sir," Rex replied. "We know they have *sayanim* in Hong Kong and mainland China. It was Hong Kong-based *sayanim* who made it possible for us to smuggle Yuan Lee out of China. Those *sayanim* and others could be of immense help to us to put tabs on the generals and get us the information we need to decide which of them, hopefully, all three, might be open to an offer from us. I'm sure the Israelis will cooperate with us and allow us to use their *sayanim*, but we'll have to ask."

Mossad is the smallest but generally regarded as the

most efficient among the world's leading intelligence agencies. Revered by their bigger counterparts and deeply feared by the enemies of Israel. Yet, notwithstanding their size, they have a global reach envied by the bigger intelligence agencies. They had devised a brilliant plan to overcome their limitations and conduct vast operations worldwide by recruiting helpers, *sayanim*, across the world.

The *sayanim* are Jewish volunteers, bankers, restauranteurs, homeowners, hoteliers, owners and managers of guest houses, rental car companies, travel agents, lawyers, doctors, nurses, journalists, CEOs of large corporates, and many others. It was estimated that across the globe, they numbered more than ten thousand. Whenever needed, they provided mission support to Mossad's covert operations. Sayanim can have dual citizenship but are often not Israeli citizens. The Jewish diaspora definitely has some benefits for the state of Israel.

Richardson looked at his boss and said, "Howard, the team and I've discussed this idea at length the last few days, and I support the plan one hundred percent. If we can pull this off, it would not only be one of the biggest intelligence coups in the history of espionage, it might also help us to head off a full-scale war with China."

Lawrence was quiet for a few thoughtful moments. "You have my support. I'll make the case to the CWC tomorrow."

The CWC consisted of the president, Director of National Intelligence, Tia Chapman, CIA Director, Howard Lawrence, FBI Director, Douglas Cole, Lauren Woods, the Secretary of State, General Sheldon Morgan, Chairman of the Joint Chiefs of Staff, and General Caiden McKnight, the commander of the US Cyber Command.

Chapter Three

THE EMISSARIES

Tel Aviv, Israel

As expected, the CWC supported John's suggestions of which allies to brief about the MK Plan. Less than twenty-four hours after receiving the go-ahead, the emissaries were on board a Gulfstream G600 private jet registered in the name of a shell company with untraceable links to the CIA. A little over seven hours later, Richardson stepped off the plane in London. Two hours after that, Christelle was dropped off in Paris, and about five hours after that, the jet was approaching Tel Aviv, Israel.

Catia hooked her arm through Rex's and leaned her head against his shoulder, staring out the window as the jet started its final descent into Lod airport. The military section of Israel's main international airport, Ben Gurion, is located twelve miles southeast of Tel Aviv.

The Gulfstream G600 is a long-range private jet with a range of 6,500 nautical miles. With a top speed of Mach 0.925, it is faster than most other long-range private jets on the market. Besides the flight crew, it has room for nine passengers, a well-stocked kitchen and bar, a surprisingly spacious shower, and a comfortable sleeping area for each passenger.

Digger was fast asleep on his own seat when the pilot made the announcement. Even though he'd never been to Israel, his ears only pitched momentarily. He sighed softly and went back to sleep. He was a frequent flyer; take-offs and landings didn't excite him anymore.

Catia, an Italian Jew, born and bred in Rome from a lineage of Jews living in the Eternal City for more than four and a half centuries, had only been to Israel a few times in her life. Her father worked for the Israeli intelligence service out of their office in Rome when he and Catia's mother were assassinated by Hezbollah; Catia was in her early twenties. After the death of her parents, Catia was recruited by Mossad and trained as a mission support specialist, and she'd worked for them until she and Rex got married a few years ago. Since then, she has had what could best be described as a freelance relationship with Mossad.

It was Rex's second visit to Israel. The last time was in 2008, about two years before meeting Catia, when he spent a day in Jerusalem to meet with a Mossad agent who had information for him about Al Qaeda.

Yaron Aderet, the man Rex and Catia came to see, was the head of Mossad's largest department, Collections, tasked with all the many aspects of conducting espionage overseas.

He was also Catia's *katsa*, the Hebrew word for handler. And he was a good friend of John Brandt since the Cold War days. As field agents, they ran joint CIA-Mossad operations against the Soviet bloc intelligence agencies and their cronies in the Middle East. Catia was like a daughter to him, and he was the man who led her down the aisle on her wedding day. He was one of the guests of honor at Brandt's and Christelle's wedding in Vietnam a few months ago.

Aderet knew Rex for as long as he had known Catia. In short, Aderet was part of the CRC family and on a sound footing with Martin Richardson. There were often situations requiring the CIA and Mossad to collaborate closely, as was the case now. Not only for the sake of Israel and the United States but for the world. After all, the Chinese ambitions didn't end with conquering America; they had a world vision.

The *Gulfstream* taxied into a hangar, the doors were closed, and the stairs deployed as soon as they came to a stop. At the bottom of the stairs, a man in his mid-thirties, in a short-sleeve khaki shirt and matching pants, waited for them. He greeted them in Hebrew, told them his name was Dan Myer, shook their hands, laughed when Digger offered his right paw and shook it, and led them to a black Mercedes SUV with tinted windows parked inside the hangar.

Half an hour later, Myer showed them into Aderet's office. His rugged face chiseled over a period of seventy-four summers in a harsh country surrounded by enemies who had only one dream—to wipe his people off the face of the earth—lit up like the lights on a Christmas tree when he saw Catia. He hugged her and then kissed her on both cheeks before shaking hands with Rex and Digger.

Although all three were fluent in English, they were conversing in Hebrew. Rex was a polyglot, capable of eight languages. He had an almost supernatural ability to learn

new languages, and a mysterious quirk was that he uncon-
sciously took on the accent of his teachers. Consequently, he
spoke Hebrew in the manner of an Italian because he
learned it from Catia.

"Come, have a seat," Aderet pointed at the coffee table
and easy chairs in the corner. "Let's have coffee and something to eat."

The first few minutes of the conversation were spent on
the usual inquiries about their flight, how they and mutual
acquaintances were doing, and suchlike.

By the time Aderet's secretary had served the refreshments and left, the personal stuff had been covered, and it
was time to talk business.

Rex opened the briefcase he had with him, retrieved a
flash drive and a stack of documents, and placed them on
the coffee table. "Those are all for you, Yaron. It's going to
take you a couple of days, if not more, to work through it
all. Catia and I will give you the condensed version now if
that's okay with you?"

"I am yours for the next three hours, then I have a
meeting with the director and the Prime Minister, which
will take the rest of the day. After that, you will have my
undivided attention again until tomorrow morning when I
have to get on a plane to Poland."

"That's more than enough time," said Catia.

"Good. I'm listening."

"It's about China," Rex started. "About three months
ago, we happened across a document containing the blueprint of how the PRC intends to fulfill Mao Tse-tung's
dream of a world under Chinese communist rule within the
next two to four years—"

Aderet was grinning when he interrupted, "Happened
across, really?"

Rex smiled and shrugged. "Yeah, that's what I've been told."

Catia was staring intently at her feet, and Digger was asleep on the floor next to her.

"O-k-a-y," said Aderet. The old spy was not fooled by Rex's or Catia's performance. "But at some stage, I'd like to hear how it happened."

"You know the protocol Yaron, we never reveal details about our sources. But John and Martin want you to know that they will share the information from the source with you."

"Thanks, that's good enough for me. Now, why was this document not brought to our attention three months ago?"

"We had no way of verifying that the document was the truth or being used to misdirect us. We had to wait and see if they'd launch the actions described in the document."

"I take it they did, and that's why you're here?"

"Yep. Step by step and word for word as in the document. I'll let Catia tell you. She was the mission control on that one."

Aderet shifted his gaze to Catia.

"The Chinese had a plan to block the Strait of Malacca by blowing up one of their own oil tankers in the narrowest part of the Phillips Channel and blame it on pirates. If they had been successful, they would have had an excuse to send their navy to take control of the strait and protect it from pirates. And, of course, it would have given them an excuse to station some of their warships there permanently. The first step in ultimately taking control of the South China Sea."

Several major sea routes provide entry into the South China Sea: the Sunda Strait, the Lombok Strait, and the Strait of Malacca, among them. The latter is the most widely used because it is the shortest and most economical passageway between the Pacific and Indian Oceans. Thus, taking control of the South China Sea would have to start by taking control of the three straits.

Catia told him, in broad strokes, how their mission was executed.

Aderet was smiling when Catia finished. "Our resources in the area passed on some information about an incident involving pirates and a Chinese oil tanker, but none of it made sense. Now it does. I love it. I don't think our Metsada could've done it any better."

The Special Operations Division of Mossad is known as Metsada, a small but lethal counterterrorism unit of special operators responsible for assassinations, paramilitary operations, sabotage, and psychological warfare.

Rex took over from Catia and, for the next two hours, gave Aderet an overview of the various operations envisaged in the MK Plan, including the incorporation of Hong Kong and Macau, the invasion of Taiwan, and fomenting more conflict in the Middle East.

"I know the details are in the documents, but would you mind expanding about their plans to stoke more trouble in the Middle East."

"They have in mind to put Saudi Arabia, the Sunnis, and Iran, the Shiites, at each other's throats. And, of course, to help radical Islam with their favorite pastime—wiping Israel off the map. On the latter, there's not much detail in the plan other than supporting Israel's enemies with money and weapons. You will, however, see a bit more details about their plans to make a pact with Iran."

"Tell me about this deal with Iran."

"Their take on it is that both China and Iran have global and regional ambitions, and both have belligerent relationships with America and Israel. So, China is looking at forming a strategic partnership in trade, politics, culture, and security with Iran. They believe it would be a win-win for both countries. They will have access to Iran's oil and gas, and Iran will get out of the stranglehold of international sanctions—"

"And get China's help to develop their nuclear weapons with which they would wipe us off the map," Aderet whispered.

"Exactly."

"Okay, so what is expected of Israel?"

"Martin was hoping we might be able to convince you to make a short trip to Langley within the next few days. He and John want to meet in person to tell you about the operation they've got going and what role Israel can play in it."

Aderet leaned back in his chair. "That shouldn't be a problem; I can go to Langley from Warsaw. But I get the impression that your trip over here was not just to hand me the documents, brief me about what the PRC is up to, and ask me to meet with Martin and John. Right?"

Rex nodded. "The main reason we're here is to ask for your help with the recruitment of three senior generals of the PLA."

Aderet's intercom buzzed. His secretary told him that the driver had arrived to take him and the director to the meeting with the Prime Minister. "I'll be there in a minute," he said, then turned to Rex and Catia and said, "I should be finished by six. Where are you staying?"

"We haven't booked in anywhere. We're planning to fly to Hong Kong after the meeting with you tonight," said Catia.

"Okay, I'll meet you here at around six, and we'll go for dinner."

Aderet was back at his office at 6:15 p.m. and took them to the Norman Hotel, where he had made a reservation at the very popular Alena restaurant. Management had no problems with Digger accompanying them to dinner. Sitting on the floor between Rex and Catia, he got his usual share of the delicacies his companions were enjoying so much. Halfway through the dinner, he had enough and went to sleep.

Rex and Catia told Aderet about their plan to recruit the three PLA generals and how three prominent Hong Kong Jews who were also *sayanim*, Jethro Matz, Tamara Matz, and David Sarlin, could help them.

Rex and Catia had met the three about a year ago when they were instrumental in the defection of General Yuan Lee from China which helped them to foil the plans of the previous Chinese president to start a biological Armageddon.

Aderet required no convincing. "Of course, we'll help. I'll call Jethro right now."

Hong Kong is six hours ahead of Tel Aviv, and Jethro Matz was not impressed when the ringing of his secured satellite phone woke him at 3:00 a.m., but his displeasure quickly made way for concern upon hearing Aderet's voice.

Although Aderet kept the conversation short and the details vague, Jethro quickly comprehended the request and agreed without hesitation to see Rex and Catia.

By 11:00 p.m. Tel Aviv time, the CIA jet was back in the air en route to Hong Kong, eleven hours away.

Chapter Four

MEETING OLD FRIENDS

Matz Island, Hong Kong

By 4:00 p.m., when the CIA jet with Rex, Catia, and Digger landed on Matz Island, Hong Kong, eleven thousand miles had been covered, and thirty-six hours had passed since they'd left D.C. The luxury of having the entire passenger cabin to themselves and comfortable sleeping amenities helped somewhat to stave off the effects of jetlag, but not all of it.

Jethro Matz, the richest man in Hong Kong and one of the richest in the world, was a Hong Kong Jew and CEO of Matz Enterprises, Hong Kong's largest electricity supplier. Matz Enterprises also owned a nuclear power station ninety miles northeast of Hong Kong. It was the sole supplier of electricity to several of South China's mega industrial plants.

Jethro and his wife and sister, Tamara, lived on their own private island, Matz Island. It was not big, maybe forty hectares, but it was spectacular. The house and outbuildings were palatial—high-security fences and guards, a runway for private jets, and a helicopter pad. Jethro's high-speed, eight-passenger Airbus H155 helicopter could reach Hong Kong's financial district in less than thirty minutes. Matz Enterprises headquarters was in the penthouse of the tallest building in Hong Kong.

David Sarlin was also a Hong Kong Jew, a close friend of Jethro, and CEO of HK Securities, a major player in the financial, banking, investment, and insurance industries. Sarlin was not as rich as the Matz family but not too far behind.

The Matz and Sarlin families' ancestors migrated from Baghdad, Iraq, to India. Then, in the early 1800s, they moved to Shanghai from where they moved to Hong Kong when it was ceded to Great Britain by China in 1842.

These days, the Jewish community of Hong Kong numbers about five thousand. They are a close-knit and dynamic society and are strongly tied to Israel. Although there were only a handful of Jewish families in Hong Kong in the mid-19th century, they enjoyed enormous success, and several became fabulously wealthy, like the Matz and Sarlin families.

A little over a year ago, a lifelong friendship was formed between the Matz and Sarlin families with the Daltons (Rex, Catia, and Digger) and the Farleys (Josh and Marissa) when they saved Tamara Matz, co-CEO of Matz Enterprises, when the Chinese triad, Sun Yee On, tried to kill her. A few days later, they rescued Doris Frankel, née Sarlin, David's sister, when the same gang abducted her, Catia, and Marissa. Those events led to the discovery of the President of China's diabolical plan to unleash a deadly virus on an unsuspecting world. But with the help of Jethro and David,

Rex and his team were able to prevent it from happening in the nick of time.

Jethro Matz, his wife, Liu, Tamara, David Sarlin, and his wife, Ren, met them at the landing strip on Matz Island. Hugs and kisses and handshakes were exchanged, and Digger got a pawshake and a head scratch from everyone.

Although Jethro and David were burning to know what brought the Daltons to Matz Island again, their wives insisted that the guests be allowed to have some refreshments first. Dinner was to be served at eight.

An hour later, Rex and Catia were in conclave with Jethro, Tamara, and David in the opulent study. Digger, who seldom missed a meeting, had decided it was more important to accompany Liu and Ren on their afternoon walk around the island. Maybe he felt he needed a bit of exercise after all the traveling. But, of course, it was also possible that his decision had something to do with the small pieces of jerky the ladies had been slipping to him since his arrival.

Jethro poured a drink for everyone and sat down in his chair. "Cheers," he toasted and took a sip. Everyone followed suit.

Although both Rex and Catia were capable of conversing in Mandarin, they preferred to speak English, in which all of them were fluent.

"So, Rex, Catia, let's cut to the chase. Yaron indicated it's a serious matter."

"Yes, and this time it's worse than the virus threat of a year ago," Rex said.

"The PRC at it again?"

"I'm afraid so. And unless we stop them, we're heading for war, full-scale—nukes and all."

John and Ollie had given Rex permission to share as

much classified information as he deemed necessary with Jethro and company. They did, however, caution him not to share any information about Flat Arrow unless it was vital for the success of their mission.

Accordingly, Rex and Catia told them about the MK Plan without divulging how they got their hands on it.

The Matzs and David Sarlin were well aware of China's global ambitions. After all, for the past few years, they'd experienced it as China negated its 1984 agreement with Britain about the transfer of authority of Hong Kong to China. Like a boa constrictor, it steadily invaded the political affairs of Hong Kong. However, this was the first time they got a detailed briefing about the PRC's plans for world domination and the timelines. It was deeply troubling, to say the least.

"So, how can we help?" David asked.

"We need information about certain high-ranking individuals in China that we want to target for recruitment," Catia replied.

"As spies?" Tamara wanted to know.

"Yes."

Just then, Liu Matz stuck her head into the study and said, "Dinner's ready."

The dinner was everything Rex and Catia thought it was going to be—a sumptuous banquet. Fortunately, they'd anticipated it and didn't eat much on the plane. Digger looked like he had arrived in canine nirvana as he was served a seemingly endless stream of a variety of meats and treats in his bowl.

A little over an hour and a half later, the five were back in Jethro's study. This time Digger honored them with his presence.

"Okay, let's get back to your request earlier," Jethro started. "Who do you have in mind?"

"Our primary target at the moment is General Lang Jianhong, commander of the PLA Ground Forces," said Rex.

"Why him?"

"Well, he is the chairman of the group of thirteen who call themselves the Trustees. They're the authors of the MK Plan—"

"The Trustees?"

"Yep, they fancy themselves as the stewards of the political power of China."

"Thirteen. Who are they?"

Catia smiled. "Hang on to your hats. General Lang, the chairman, as Rex said. Liao Qigang, the president. Tao Huan, the Chairman of the Central Military Commission. General Dai Min, whom you know very well. General Wan Huang of the Air Force, the man who helped Dai with the defection of General Yuan. General Jin Ping in charge of Information Operations and Information Warfare, the cyber warfare division of the PLA. Admiral Deng Jie, the commander of the People's Liberation Army Navy, as well as Generals Xia Wei, Kong Yuhan, Zeng Jiahao, Wu Shuren, and Vice-Admiral Shao Yong, commander of the PLA submarine fleet."

"Ten marshals, the president, and the head of the military," whispered David. "It can't get more high-ranking and sinister than that. Who is number thirteen?"

"That one is a bit of a mystery," said Rex. He's referred to in the plan as Zhì Zhě, which I believe is the Mandarin word for Wise Man?"

"Yes, it is," said Tamara. "So, obviously, Liao Qigang

and Tao Huan are the puppets of those ten marshals who would've put them into their positions."

What very few people outside the Communist Party's inner circles knew was that the president and anyone else in the top positions in the country were actually beholden to the marshals. There were seventeen of them. They were generals of the PLA who were not controlled by, nor were they part of the PRC government. They were part of the Chinese Communist Party (CCP).

"By the way, do any of you believe that Li Lingxin died from a heart attack?" Asked Rex.

Everyone smiled and shook their heads. "Not a chance," said David. "I'd say he died from a bullet wound, which could very well have been self-inflicted."

Rex nodded. "Yeah, that's the general consensus among us as well."

"I've met all of the so-called Trustees, except of course the mystery man, Zhì Zhě," said Jethro. "What is perplexing, though, is that Dai and Wan are among them. A year ago, they feared a confrontation with America. But now, they're enthusiastically working on a plan to start a world war. What has changed?"

"We also found that strange," said Rex, "but thus far, we've got no logical explanation. Hopefully, Lang can cast some light on the subject."

"What makes you think that General Lang might be recruitable?" asked Jethro.

Rex had to tread carefully not to reveal information about Flat Arrow yet make sure he didn't offend their hosts. "We have reason to believe that Lang is hiding some critical information from his co-trustees. Which, if it were to come to light, would earn him a bullet in the back of the head. We think he's a worried man, which might make him susceptible to suggestions of how to get out of his predicament. So, what we're after is information about Lang's life and routine —comprehensive surveillance. We hope to get information that would put us in a position to make an approach."

The room went quiet for a long while before Jethro spoke. "Yes, I think it's possible. We will put our heads together and come up with a plan of action. We should be able to get something going within the next day or two."

"Thank you," said Rex and Catia in chorus.

"I take it the wayward generals, Dai and Wan are the secondary targets?" asked Tamara.

"Indeed," said Rex.

"I've been wondering about their change of heart," mused David. "A year ago, the PLA was not ready for the inevitable war that would have followed the release of that virus. Although, unless they've developed some kind of secret superweapon, I don't think China's military power has changed so much that they're now ready to challenge the world."

"The MK Plan makes no mention of a secret weapon," said Rex.

Jethro knew Dai Min very well. The general was in charge of the PLA's Rocket Force, sixteen brigades of China's nuclear and conventional strategic missiles. Ex officio, he was a board member of the Matz Enterprises subsidiary company, which owned the nuclear power station ninety miles northeast of Hong Kong. "How do you want to handle the two of them?" Jethro asked.

"The same as Lang. We need all the information about them we can get. The thing is, we suspect that Dai and Wan never told the Trustees or anyone exactly how the defection of Yuan Lee went down and how they've actually collaborated with the CIA during that mission. Between yourselves, us, and the information collected during Yuan's debriefing, we have the precise details, and that gives us potential leverage over them."

"Good. We'll do the same as for Lang," said Jethro.

By eleven o'clock, Rex and Catia could not to keep their eyes open any longer, made their excuses, and went to bed.

Jethro, Tamara, and David continued the meeting throughout the night. Over breakfast the next morning, they told Rex and Catia about their plans to put the targets under surveillance.

By 10:30 a.m. Rex, Catia, and Digger boarded the CIA jet for the 8,000-mile seventeen-hour trip back to D.C.

Chapter Five

DECEPTION OVER DINNER

Langley, Virginia, USA

A deceptive tactic used by spy agencies is to send one of their agents as a fake defector into the enemy camp. During the Cold War, the Russians were exceptionally good at it. The defector would be a disinformation agent who could create havoc. This included telling his hosts that one or more of their own people have been spying for their enemy or provide false information that the hosts would act upon. Spy agencies know this and have protocols in place to root out fake defectors. But it is a long and tedious process that requires months of interrogation, checking, and double-checking the veracity of the information provided by the defector.

The Peregrine team didn't have a fake defector to send into the Chinese camp. But they had someone who could do as much or more damage to the PRC's spy industry as a fake defector. Her codename was Stardust, and her real name Jordyn Lancaster, the senior senator from New York.

She was fifty-four but looked thirty. She was beautiful—very beautiful—in the same way an iceberg was beautiful. And equally forbidding. She struck a stately figure—the epitome of elegance and possessed a razor-sharp mind. It was a lethal combination of attributes she had put to good use in the cutthroat world of Washington, D.C. politics.

She was very wealthy; her grandfather made a fortune in the oil industry. Her father was a real estate mogul, and she inherited it all. As a Harvard Law School graduate, she was welcomed into New York state politics fresh out of the university. By the age of thirty-three, she took her seat in the US Senate and was now in her third six-year term. What she craved now was the most intoxicating narcotic known to mankind: power—the kind of power only a president had. The media loved her because she was well-spoken, livened up their audiences with her alluring beauty, and hated the current president with a passion. "Exactly the type of personality the American people deserved as their president in times like these," they would often say.

She was the chairperson of the Senate Committee on Foreign Relations. The Committee was tasked with leading foreign-policy legislation, funding foreign aid programs, as well as arms sales to and training for allied countries. Her committee was also responsible for the confirmation hearings for high-level positions in the Department of State. It was her position on this podium that put her and the president at loggerheads on a perpetual basis. Among them was the disagreement about relations with China. The president started the trade war with them and made it clear that he firmly believed China was a threat to national security. Lancaster, on the contrary, was advocating for better relations and open trade agreements.

And Beijing loved her for it.

The MSS knew that senators and representatives were regularly privy to top-secret information. That's why the MSS had dedicated a team of analysts and undercover agents to study the life and habits of Senator Jordyn Lancaster.

Once they thought they had enough information about her, they sent a male honey trap to seduce her and filmed the whole affair. A week or two later, they introduced her to Song Yuhan, a Chinese national working in the Cultural Office of the Chinese Consulate General in New York. According to Song, his job was "to promote China-U.S. cultural and tourism exchange and cooperation, promoting mutual understanding, mutual learning, and friendship between our countries." It was a lie; he was an MSS agent, and he was going to be her handler. She was from now on in their hands. She would spy for the MSS, or they would destroy her.

But the Peregrine counterintelligence team and Senator Lancaster knew different. The MSS had no idea what a consummate actor the senator was. Hence, they had no idea that the senator had received a defensive briefing from the counterintelligence team two days after her first encounter with the MSS honey trap and that she'd been working closely with them since. Thus, that night when Song Yuhan thought he had recruited her to spy for the PRC, he was actually the one who had been recruited.

New York, USA

Two weeks after the 'recruitment' of Senator Lancaster, she and Song Yuhan met at the Le Bernardin. The elite French restaurant on 155 W 51st Street, New York, was the venue for the handover of the first tranche of information.

Song was already at the table, which he had reserved a few days before. He was, however, completely unaware of the mini-microphones and mini-video cameras placed in strategic but entirely invisible positions.

Lancaster was fifteen minutes late. It was deliberate. She had to keep up the ruse of being deeply offended by the way Song had coerced her into spying for the Chinese communist regime.

Song made no mention of her unpunctuality; he stood when she approached. "Good evening, Senator. How kind of you to join me." He pulled a chair out for her.

She sat down. "Song, don't patronize me. We both know I'm here because I have no choice."

"Senator, I just wish you wouldn't be so antagonistic about all of this. You've always propagated for better relations between our countries which is why we've chosen to work with you. We both know how much damage this president has done to the good relations that always existed between us. He's been pushing the world into war. You're now in a position where you—"

"Listen, I told you not to patronize me. You're a damn spy, and you're blackmailing me—"

"Senator, I'm not proud of the method that the MSS has used in this case. But sometimes, distasteful methods have to be employed for the greater good. We, the PRC, that is, want you in the Oval Office. The American people want you in the Oval Office. The world will be much better off and a much safer place with you as the President of the United States."

Lancaster suppressed a grin as she thought how much she was going to enjoy pulling the rug from under this egomaniacal idiot's feet one day. But, in the interim, she had to bite her tongue and play the game. "Well, so far, you've given me no reason to believe that you will live up to your promises. Meanwhile, I'm the one running the risk of being caught and charged with treason."

"It's early days, Senator. It will happen. And no one is going to accuse you of treason for meeting with the Chinese Cultural attaché."

"You know, Song, there are times when I'm seriously tempted to resign and move to another country."

"Of course, that's your prerogative to do so. But I'm sure you won't."

"Yeah, and why not?"

"Your intellect and your ambitions. You *know* that you're one of the most intelligent people in Congress. You *know* that you've got what it takes to be the leader of this country and to be the most powerful person in the world. And most of all, you believe that it will never be done properly unless you're doing it yourself."

"Oh, excuse me, I didn't know you're also a psychoanalytic expert." Lancaster's sarcasm belied her surprise at how accurate Song was and how scary it was to see how much they knew about her. She couldn't help but think about what an unbearable position she would've been in if the FBI didn't discover the Chinese plot. She took a small USB flash drive out of her handbag and pushed it across the table next to Song's wineglass.

When he brought the glass to his lips to take a sip, the flash drive had disappeared.

Lancaster told him it contained the transcripts of all the foreign policy legislation currently being debated in her committee as he had requested.

In the ops room, John, Ollie, and Lydia Andrews, the

FBI liaison officer seconded to Operation Peregrine, were smiling. It was classified information that Lancaster had passed on to Song. However, it was of such a nature that China would not be able to use it in any manner that could harm the interests of the United States. And the Chinese probably knew it would be useless information. But that was not the reason the MSS requested it in the first place. Their primary objective was to get Senator Lancaster to cross the Rubicon—to commit an incontrovertible act of espionage for China. That would give them the most powerful leverage possible over her. Much, much more powerful than the videotapes of her tryst with their honeytrap.

And that was precisely what John Brandt and Ollie Campbell wanted them to believe. They were pleasantly surprised when Song Yuhan made his next request immediately after receiving the flash drive. They thought he would want to study the contents of the drive before placing his next order. Even so, they were not overly worried; Ollie and Lydia had prepared the senator well.

"You're good friends with several members of the House Intelligence Committee, are you not?"

The Intelligence Committee is the primary committee in the U.S. House of Representatives responsible for oversight of the United States intelligence community. It shares some jurisdiction with other committees, such as the Armed Services Committee for matters dealing with the Department of Defense and the various branches of the U.S. military. This committee handled highly classified information. The kind of information America's enemies would do almost anything to get access to. The committee members and their staff always understood how important it was to maintain the highest levels of security. But sad as it was, the committee came under intense scrutiny over the last few

years due to allegations of partisanship and leaks of classified information.

"Yes. Why... Wait a minute, you can put that out of your
mind right now. I'm not spying on my friends. Unlike you, I
have a conscience, I won't bribe or blackmail any of them,
I'll give you every bit of information going through my
hands or coming to my ears, but I won't descend to your
level—"

"I think you've missed an important milestone tonight,
Senator." Song interrupted and leaned forward while he
spoke. "When you handed me that flash drive, you've
crossed the line. You're now a spy for the PRC. You see,
until tonight, all we had were those embarrassing videos
that could destroy your career. Besides destroying your
career and embarrassing you, we could also see to it that
you spend the rest of your life inside a maximum-security
prison. So, I suggest you reconsider."

Lancaster went quiet. She swallowed. Through clenched
teeth, she hissed, "What do you want?"

"The transcripts of their meetings, all of them."

"Impossible. It will be discovered quickly, and I'd be
exposed. Moreover, I don't know how their security protocols work. It's too dangerous."

"Well, then it's your job to find out exactly how they
work. And in the meantime, I want you to get a copy of the
transcript of the debriefing of General Yuan Lee, who
defected to America a year ago. You've heard about him,
haven't you?"

Thanks to Ollie, the senator knew exactly who General
Yuan Lee was, but she played dumb. "Never heard of him,
but I'll see what I can find."

Chapter Six

THE AIDE AND THE DRIVER

Beijing, China

Soon after starting their inquiries into General Lang, through their contacts inside the Chinese Communist Party (CCP), Jethro and David learned that many of those in the upper echelons of power in the CCP were nothing if not gossipmongers. A surprising number thought of President Liao as a weakling. That Tao Huan had presidential aspirations. And in the same circles, they've heard whispers about General Lang's self-aggrandizing style and his drinking problem.

Continuing their surreptitious queries, they also got the names of Lang's *aide-de-camp* and driver and, of course, the inevitable gossip about them.

The *aide-de-camp* was Colonel Dong Qui. And he was a serious gambler. But since the Communist Party took power in 1949, any form of gambling by Chinese citizens, even if they were outside the borders of China, was strictly forbidden. However, law enforcement authorities turned a blind eye when certain privileged Chinese citizens gambled in Macau. The biggest gambling center in the world since 2007 when Macau overtook the Las Vegas Strip in gaming revenues.

After his promotion to colonel, Dong was more than just a little miffed to find out he still didn't count among the privileged. It didn't stop him, though, from dreaming and talking about visiting the casinos of Macau at least once in his life. Therefore, until that day arrived, he had to satisfy his gambling urges by participating in the one trillion yuan (about $154 billion) illegal gambling industry inside China, which included unofficial lotteries, clandestine casinos, and putting money down in games such as mahjong and various card games.

Dong was living dangerously, and he knew it. It was not only his career that would come to an end if he got caught; he was also facing a lengthy jail sentence.

Lang's driver was Corporal Adil Tursun. He was 57, the son of a dirt-poor Uyghur peasant family from the Xinjiang area in the northwest of the country, officially known as Xinjiang Uyghur Autonomous Region. The region is home to several ethnic groups, including the Kazakhs, Kyrgyz, the Han, Tibetans, Hui, Tajiks, Mongols, Russians, Xibe, and the Uyghurs. For decades hundreds of thousands of Uyghur Muslims have been singled out by the government and interned in camps as punishment for their religious or cultural expression. The Chinese government also used draconian measures to slash birth rates among Uyghurs and other minorities to curb the region's Muslim population.

Although Adil was Uyghur, he was not a Muslim, neither was his family. That and the fact that he was an intelligent, diligent, and loyal man helped to get him into the People's Liberation Army. However, it didn't protect him from discrimination on account of his ethnicity. After more than thirty years of service, he had received only one promotion, from private to private first class. Two years ago, at the age of fifty-five, he received his second and final promotion. He was now a corporal and a general's driver—the commander of the PLA's ground force, no less. A job that was "An honor and a privilege to have," as his superior, who gave him the promotion, told him.

Adil had three years until retirement from a lifetime of disappointment and humiliation. For him, the last two years as General Lang's driver, the job which was supposed to be an honor and a privilege to have, was the worst of all his time in the military. General Lang was a rude, self-centered man and a bigot. After two years, he still addressed Adil as "driver" because he couldn't be bothered to remember his name.

It didn't take much to get confirmation that the rumor mill was remarkably accurate about the lives of Dong Qui and Adil Tursun.

Dong was indeed a habitual gambler, though not good at it. Lady Luck must have taken a serious dislike in him since he had racked up more than 200,000 yuan (about $30,000) in debt the past few months. And the loansharks were circling.

As for Adil, he was indeed as disgruntled as the rumors suggested.

Jethro passed all of this information on to Yaron Aderet via the secured communications link, who promptly passed it to John Brandt.

Three days later, Rex, Catia, and Digger arrived in Beijing on an Air France flight from Paris on their French EU passports as Rowan and Catherine Donnelly for a short vacation.

Chapter Seven

THE GAMBLER

Beijing, China

The venue for tonight's poker game was in one of the back rooms of a small house in a poor neighborhood on the north-side of Beijing in what was known as a *hutong*, a narrow alleyway formed by traditional courtyard houses. The subway station was less than a mile away. In fact, the house was less than a fifteen-minute walk from the house where Colonel Dong Qui and a guard tortured an old lady, General Lang's office cleaner, to death a few months ago.

Her crime? She had stolen candy from a bowl on the general's desk. She had no idea that one of the items she took from the bowl was a USB memory stick containing top-secret information. The old lady told them that she'd given the 'candy' to her four-year-old granddaughter, but the child and her parents and the memory stick had disappeared without a trace. Ever since, General Lang, who by nature was near-impossible to work for, had become insufferable.

But neither General Lang nor the old lady was on Dong's mind when he entered the gambling house that night. He had 7,000 yuan (a little over $1,000) in his pocket, debt amounting to 200,000 yuan, and three extremely bad-tempered loan sharks looking for him. He was a desperate man but totally unaware that he had been under surveillance for a few days already.

Dong noticed that the homeowner was uncharacteristically aloof when he greeted him at the door and led him to the room where three round tables had been set up. No one else was in attendance yet.

"Have a seat. The others should be here soon. Help yourself to some tea in the meantime," the owner said as he left and closed the door behind him.

Dong poured himself a cup of tea, sat down at one of the tables, retrieved a packet of Marlboro cigarettes from his jacket pocket, took one out, and lit it.

As he blew out a cloud of smoke, the door opened. An unknown Asian male in his mid-thirties, about five-foot-eleven in height, with penetrating dark eyes, the physique of a gymnast, and a stern-looking facial expression, entered the room. Following him was a mean-looking big black dog, unleashed. The dog walked around the table and sat two paces away from Dong's left side.

Dong drew a sharp breath and almost choked on the smoke still in his mouth. He knew trouble when he saw it. There was not going to be any gambling tonight. This man was, without doubt, the loansharks' enforcer. Dong had seen many enforcers since he took up gambling. He even had a physical encounter with one of them once—an unforgettable experience. Enforcers were big powerful men, bald heads, lots of tattoos, chain-smokers, and merciless. They were scary people. This man looked nothing like them, yet, somehow, he was orders of magnitude more intimidating than the most menacing enforcer Dong had ever seen.

When Dong's coughing fit subsided, the man said, "You should quit. Those things are bad for your health."

Dong was gawking at the man who spoke in the Beijing dialect, known as Pekingese, the prestige dialect of Mandarin spoken in the urban area of Beijing. Finally, he regained some composure and said, "Who the hell are you?"

The big black dog growled softly. As if to say, "Don't talk to my friend in that tone." The dog had a weird look on his face, his tongue was hanging out, and his lips were curled up at the corners. If Dong would've asked the man about the look, the man would've told him the dog was annoyed. It would have been a lie. The dog was experienced in the interrogation of bad guys. At the moment, he was enjoying the whole charade very much. The look on his face was the canine version of a smile.

The man said, "For purposes of the conversation we're about to have, it's not important who I am—"

"Do you have any idea who I am?"

The dog shifted his gaze from his owner to Dong and snarled.

Dong was getting nervous; it was as if this damn dog understood everything that was said.

The man looked at the dog and asked, "What's this guy's name?"

The dog let out a loud yelp.

The man nodded and said, "My dog says you're Colonel Dong Qui, the *aide-de-camp* of General Lang Jian-hong, commander of the PLA Ground Force. Right?"

Dong's eyes were wide shot. When he spoke, his gaze

was flicking between the man and the dog. "I... don't have the money, I... I... need more time I..."

"Then I'm going to give you ten reasons you'll never forget this meeting—"

The dog growled.

"Wait! I... Please... just one week... I'm begging you... please!"

"Time's up. You owe my employers two hundred thousand. You've already had two extensions. If you have no money, I'm to take your fingers in lieu of payment. Twenty thousand per finger."

The man took a Swiss Army knife out of his pocket and placed it on the table.

Dong's eyes bulged. His face was white as paper. He reached into his jacket pocket, took the 7,000 yuan out, and placed it on the table. "That's all I have... I..."

The man shook his head slowly, and the dog started snarling and growling softly. The enforcer picked the knife up, opened the saw blade, looked at Dong for a few beats as if he had just remembered something. "You know what, I just had a thought. There might be another way to do this; you might even keep your fingers, or at least some of them. Want to hear my idea?"

Dong nodded vigorously. "Yes! Please."

"Okay, I want to hear everything there is to know about General Lang Jianhong."

Dong was thunderstruck. He opened his mouth, closed it, finally managed to get it open again, and said, "Who are you? What about my debt? Why—"

"Dong, the information or your fingers?"

It soon became apparent that Dong loved his fingers infinitely more than the whiskey-guzzling, bad-mannered general. For the next two hours, Colonel Dong told Rex everything he knew about General Lang, including how the general lost a red USB flash drive with top-secret information on it. And about the general's courtesan.

The information about the mistress or courtesan as Dong called her immediately gave Rex an idea.

However, when Dong got to the part about killing the old cleaning lady, and he tried to skirt around it, Rex had to mobilize an inordinate amount of restraint not to immediately avenge Sun Jia's death, the mother of Sun Yan, code-named Flat Arrow.

Hours later, when the door closed behind the fearsome anonymous man with the forbidding dark eyes and the menacing black dog, Colonel Dong let out a long sigh of relief. He still had all his fingers and his job, and as long as he was not caught spying on his boss, his life would not be in danger. This man's employer had bought all his gambling debt which meant his financial troubles were over, but so were his gambling days and his dreams of Macau.

Dong had no way of knowing that throughout the meeting, both the man and his dog were rigged with communications gear relaying everything to the man's wife sitting in a Honda SUV parked a few hundred yards away.

However, what Dong knew full well was that losing his fingers, his job, and his life, in that order, was definitely in the cards if he dared renege on any part of their agreement. He shivered at the thought of a bullet penetrating his skull. He would talk to the general's courtesan as he was told to do. He had installed the GPS tracking app on his mobile phone while the man was watching and would install the same app on the general's phone first thing in the morning. And he would do everything else expected of him in the future.

Beijing, China

Back in their hotel room, Catia helped Rex remove the makeup she had put on to disguise him as an Asian male. Afterward, they ordered room service and listened to the recording over a late-night snack. Digger got his food in his bowl and his kong stuffed to the brim with peanut butter, or as Catia called it, Digger's gelato, and retired to the couch for the night.

"I don't think we need the help of the driver anymore," said Catia when the recording ended.

Rex agreed. "The driver won't know more than Dong. If we find out he does, then we can pay him a visit. Let's talk about Lang's mistress—"

"Courtesan," Catia corrected. "They're not mistresses; they're trained professionals."

"Sounds like you've done a bit of research, Doctor Romano?" Catia's maiden name was Romano, and she had a Ph.D. in history from the Sapienza University of Rome.

"Not much more than a few articles I read online while waiting for you to finish with Dong."

"Well, that's much more than I know. Care to tell me?"

She smiled. "Okay, let's take a shower and get into bed. I'll tell you before we go to sleep."

"But I actually had—"

Catia laughed when she placed her finger on Rex's lips, "something else in mind," she completed the sentence for him.

Rex nodded.

"So do I. The lecture won't take long."

She didn't lie; it took only a few minutes.

Most people know about the Japanese geisha girls. However, few know that the name and tradition originated in China more than 2,500 years ago. Unlike modern prostitutes who only perform sexual acts for money, the courtesans, as they were called in China, were professionally trained in the arts of music and dance. During the three hundred years of the Ming dynasty (1368-1644), they were known to be elegant and talented women, called *mingji*. They were educated in music, poetry, painting, calligraphy, and, of course, pleasing a man in the bedroom. Their clients, wealthy businessmen, high officials, learned scholars, and prominent monks competed for their favors. Women from all levels of society envied them, imitating their haughty mannerisms, elegant clothes, and elaborate hairstyles.

Although the Japanese geisha has survived, the profession of the Chinese courtesan seems to have disappeared into the recesses of history. Or so most people believe.

Despite Mao Tse-tung's claims that all forms of prostitution had been eradicated and that prostitution remains illegal in China, *jinu*, prostitutes who sell only their bodies, abound in modern-day China. It has become associated with organized crime and government corruption.

Nonetheless, in secret, the profession of the courtesan still exists today. It simply changed to keep up with the demands of modern society. The modern-day courtesan is a symbol of wealth and power to the man who could afford her. In a country where men vastly outnumber women, it is a status symbol to have two wives: a wife and a concubine. It aggrandizes the image of masculinity and power of a man in need of an ego boost.

Catia smiled as she finished. "Apparently, there's an old

Chinese saying that goes like this: *Nanren youwei cai bao er nai*, it means a man of promise will contract a second wife."

"Hmm, so Lang is a man with an ego problem, it seems," said Rex.

"Well, I believe you're also a man of promise. I'm wondering if you're in need of an ego boost?"

Rex chuckled. "With you by my side? Never. You've given me enough ego to last many lifetimes."

Catia was laughing when she threw her arms around her husband and started kissing him.

Chapter Eight

INITIATE THE TAIWAN OPERATION

Beijing, China

In a secured room in Zhongnanhai, the Chinese equivalent of the White House, about twelve miles from where the Daltons were sleeping, the Trustees had been in conference since six o'clock that afternoon. They were debating the plan to invade Taiwan, whether to proceed at this stage or not. The Trustees were well-aware of the history of Taiwan but chose to ignore it as the PRC had been doing for more than seven decades.

Humans had been inhabiting the island of Taiwan for thousands of years. Evidence of agricultural activities dates back to 3000 BC. The Dutch had colonized the island in the 17th century. This was followed by an influx of immigrants from the Fujian and Guangdong areas of mainland China. The Spanish tried to get a foothold in the north of the country but were driven out by the Dutch. In 1662 the Dutch were sent packing by Koxinga, a loyalist of the Ming dynasty, who, in turn, got defeated by the Qing dynasty in

1683. . At the end of the First Sino-Japanese War in 1895, the Qing dynasty ceded the island and Penghu to the Empire of Japan.

Japan ruled the island until the end of World War II, in 1945, when the nationalist government of the Republic of China (ROC), led by the Kuomintang (KMT), took control of Taiwan. In 1949, the KMT lost control of mainland China to Mao Tse-tung's Chinese Communist Party in the Chinese Civil War. The KMT, led by General Chiang Kai-shek and 1.2 million followers, withdrew to Taiwan and declared martial law.

In the 1950s, Mao Tse-tung's red armies moved to conquer all lost Imperial possessions and bring them under Communist rule. That included Taiwan, Tibet, and Xinjiang. His troops tried but failed to take Taiwan, which, at the end of the brutal Chinese civil war, had become the last outpost of the former Nationalist government and its supporters.

Ever since, Beijing had labeled Taiwan a renegade province, ignoring the historical fact that Taiwan was never a part of the People's Republic of China and had functioned as an independent political entity for more than seven decades.

Until the early 1970s, the Republic of China, under the KMT, was considered the only legitimate government of China by the United Nations. Most Western nations refused to recognize the People's Republic of China because of their communist government. The KMT ruled Taiwan until the late 1980s. Their stated goal was to guard against communist infiltration and prepare to retake mainland China from the communists. The KMT ruled Taiwan (and the islands of Kinmen, Wuqiu, and the Matsu on the opposite side of the Taiwan Strait) as a single-party state for forty years. Democratic reforms in the 1980s led to the first-ever direct presidential election in 1996.

However, since the end of the Cold War and the fall of communism in the Soviet Bloc countries, Taiwan had lost its membership of the United Nations to the People's Republic of China (PRC). As a result, it also lost its country status.

The PRC bluntly refused to form diplomatic relations with any countries that recognize the ROC. It was dismayed that Taiwan maintains official diplomatic relations with 14 out of 193 United Nations member states and the Holy See. And to add insult to injury, Taiwan is a member of the World Trade Organization, Asia-Pacific Economic Cooperation, and the Asian Development Bank. In addition, many countries maintain unofficial diplomatic ties with Taiwan through representative offices and institutions that function as de facto embassies and consulates.

Notwithstanding China's claims that Taiwan is Chinese territory and frequent threats of invasion and attempts to subvert Taiwan's democracy, pushing Taiwan out of international forums and bodies, and delegitimizing the state, China is still the top destination for Taiwan's exports and outbound investment.

Lately, however, Taiwan has started weaning itself from China with the introduction of the New Southbound Policy (NSP). This initiative aims to enhance cooperation and exchange between Taiwan and 18 countries in Southeast Asia, South Asia, and Australasia.

Over the past three years, Taiwan's trade with NSP countries grew from $95.8 billion to over $111 billion. As a result, outbound investment to NSP countries increased by 16 percent year-on-year. Meanwhile, outbound investment from Taiwan in China fell dramatically by 51 percent.

And the PRC didn't like that at all.

But the Trustees' problem was a military one; any attempts to move against Taiwan were sure to be met with strong countermeasures from the USA and its allies.

Although, since 1979, the USA's position on Taiwan is that the country's legal status has yet to be determined. They are steadfast in their views that Taiwan is not part of China and enacted that in the Taiwan Relations Act (TRA).

The act doesn't guarantee that the USA would intervene militarily if the PRC attacks Taiwan, but it doesn't relinquish the right to do so either. The act states that 'the United States will make available to Taiwan such defense articles and defense services in such quantity as may be necessary to enable Taiwan to maintain sufficient self-defense capabilities.' This policy had been called 'strategic ambiguity.' Nonetheless, it had thus far served to dissuade Taiwan from a unilateral declaration of independence and the PRC from unilaterally unifying Taiwan with the PRC.

Even though the USA had not based military forces in Taiwan since 1979, the Trustees knew full well that the United States was legally obligated to help defend the island country.

Until recently, the constant presence of American naval forces in Taiwan's waters was a deterrent to the PRC. But that had changed. The PLA's 1,300 medium-range missiles and their Navy's new submarines had turned the Taiwan Strait into a no-go zone for large US Navy formations.

Even so, the reality was, to invade Taiwan could mean war. For that reason, the Trustees decided to up the ante by running a series of false flag operations in Taiwan to create a climate suitable for an invasion.

During the discussions, President Liao gave his usual word of warning about the deteriorating state of the economy and his reservations about the wisdom of acts of aggression against Taiwan as it would, in all likelihood, lead to intensification of the trade war and the introduction of crippling international sanctions against the PRC. The last thing the PRC's economy needed right now.

But the rest of the Trustees had a different view. Probably because they thought that Liao had been crying wolf about the economy for so long, they just didn't believe him anymore. According to them, even if it were as bad as he suggested, the only way out was to control the world as soon as possible.

"In other words," said General Dai Min in summary, "we'll tighten our belts and ride it out. Of course, it might get worse before it gets better. But in the end, we'll emerge stronger than ever before, and we'll never have to worry about economic issues again—we'll control it all."

If everything goes according to plan... But we know it never does, The President thought.

Chapter Nine

THE GENERAL'S COURTESAN

Beijing, China

She was in her late-forties, graceful, beautiful, and sophisticated. Her name was Feng Lin. She was intelligent, educated, well-read, sympathetic, and above all, a good listener. The latter being one of her traits which Lang liked most. She instilled so much trust in him; he shared everything, even top-secret information. He absolutely believed that Lin would never talk about it. So, she listened to his problems, and she gave him comfort and advice.

Lang paid her a generous monthly stipend, as well as the rent of her cozy two-bedroom house and the utility bills. Another of her many good traits, which Lang appreciated, was that she never asked uncomfortable questions.

If the courtesans had a guild, Feng Lin would have been their poster girl and leader. But Lin was also wise enough to realize that she would never be anything other than Lang's courtesan. The 'contract' between them would end sooner or later, if not through his or her death or illness, then because of her age or her not being useful to him anymore. If she were a decade or so younger, she wouldn't have spent as much time thinking about the future as she did lately. She knew she couldn't do anything about growing older. All she could do was to keep her general happy and alive and in good health for as long as possible. And in that, she had succeeded thus far. Lang had been enamored with her for a little more than five years already and showed no signs that he was tired of her.

It troubled her that lately, her general had been drinking much more than always. He visited her more often but talked much less than before. She knew something worried him. She mentioned it. And he admitted it. She didn't ask why; he would tell her when he was ready; in the meantime, she could only do her job—help him to relax. But although she had always been able to placate him, this time, nothing seemed to work, and it bothered her that he didn't talk about it.

She knew who Colonel Dong was. She'd met him on a few occasions, but they had never socialized. Therefore, she was immediately alarmed when he turned up on her doorstep without an appointment that Friday afternoon. General Lang spent one weekend a month with her, and this was going to be their weekend together.

Dong had what she thought to be a distraught look on his face. Her first thoughts were that it was bad news about her general. He couldn't make it this weekend. He had an accident, heart attack, death, were the thoughts flashing through her mind. But then she noticed that Dong looked extremely nervous, desperate even, but not shocked or sad. She invited him in and took him to the kitchen, where she offered him tea. General Lang wasn't expected for at least another three hours.

Dong hemmed and hawed for a while when Lin asked him about the reason for his surprise visit. When he finally got to it, Lin regretted ever asking. Within a quarter of an hour, her hitherto relatively carefree life had become immensely complex. Actually, extremely dangerous.

Now she knew what had been tormenting her lover and benefactor the past few months. He was in serious trouble, the kind that could end his career in disgrace and his life in the manner that the lives of traitors ended in China—a bullet in the back of the head. And anyone associated with him, if not executed with him, would become persona non grata, outcasts, beggars on the streets if not life-long prisoners.

Dong had explained that there was only one way to escape from this nightmare. But just thinking of what was expected of her was petrifying.

She asked Dong why he didn't discuss it with Lang in person. He told her that the general would have him killed if he dared to talk to him about it. No, the only person who could save the three of them now was she.

It took her a little while to grasp all of it and realize she had only two options, abandon Lang or take her chances and help him. If it worked, it would help her as well. Abandoning him would not help her much when the MSS came for her, and she had little doubt they would. They always did, eventually.

Amid the angst, Lin had a moment or two when she became outraged about the mess General Lang had dragged her into but realized anger wouldn't solve the problem. It was too late to change anything. All she could do was what Dong had suggested and hope everything worked out.

Beijing, China

She did everything that was expected of her when Lang arrived. But it was not easy. In her profession, openness, friendliness, sociability, and elegance were essential attributes to be successful. Lang Jianhong was no prize when it came to looks. He was overweight, short, nearly bald, and his face was red from too much drinking. He had an offensive countenance, but Lin had always met it with nothing other than a pleasant demeanor.

Lang had arrived shortly after six, and the moment he set foot in the apartment, he detected that something was wrong. He didn't hug or kiss her as he always did; he immediately demanded, "What's wrong?" Before she could answer, he had pushed past her and walked to the living room, where he found his *aide de camp* sitting in *his* easy chair. He stopped in his tracks, glanced back at Lin, and snarled, "What's the meaning of this?"

Dong had jumped out of the chair and stood at attention. Before he could say a word, Lin took Lang's arm and nudged him gently into the room. "Please come and have a seat Jianhong, we've got very important matters to discuss."

Lang refused to sit. Lin took a seat. Dong moved far away from the easy chair but remained on his feet.

Lin didn't say anything; she stared Lang down. It took almost a minute before he relented and slumped down in *his* chair. Then she started talking.

The conversation that followed went through several stages of emotion. Dong remained quiet unless he was answering questions. Lin started off in her usual composed and friendly manner, often punctuated by outbursts of rage from Lang.

Lin told him about Dong Qui's gambling. Lang knew

about it; he also liked to gamble from time to time. But he knew nothing about Dong's mountain of debt. That caused his first outburst.

Next, she told him about the visit Dong received from a man with a big black dog and the demand to talk to Lang about a top-secret document that had gone missing from Lang's office.

At this juncture, Lang looked as if he was on the verge of a heart attack. "The document was stolen from the safe in my office. The cleaner did it. Her son took the documents from her, killed his own mother, and disappeared. He and his family. It was all over the news—"

Lin held her hand up. "Jianhong, I know what was in the news. But I don't know if I can believe that. You see, this mysterious man with the dog told Qui a different story, and Qui confirmed it to be correct."

Lang glowered at his aide. He turned back to Lin. "What was his story?"

Lin continued. "Apparently, the secret document was on a red USB flash drive, not in your safe but in the candy bowl on your desk. The cleaner seemed to have mistaken it for candy, took it, and gave it to her grandchild. A day or so later, you discovered the flash drive was missing, figured out the cleaner took it, and sent Qui and one of your guards to retrieve it from her. They tortured the old woman to death. But she didn't have it anymore, and you put the false story out to the press.

"That's what this man told Qui. Is that the truth or not?"

Lang's face was ashen when he turned to Dong. "You have thirty seconds to explain how this man knows what only you and I know."

Dong was still standing. He swallowed. "I can't, sir. I have no idea how that's possible—"

"You told him! That's how. You've betrayed me and your country, Dong. And I'm going to have you shot for that!"

"No, sir. I didn't. I swear to you on my mother's grave, I've never seen this man before last night. I've never talked to anyone but you about this. And he mentioned things that I have no knowledge of..."

"Such as?"

"He told me he had read the document—"

"Of course, he would have said that! How stupid are you?"

Lin got up, poured a double shot of whiskey into a glass, added ice, and placed it on the side table next to Lang.

Dong continued. "Sir, he also said that you're part of a group of thirteen people who call themselves the Trustees. He told me he knows the names of all twelve."

Lang looked as if he was about to throw up. "Did he give you any names?" His tone turned to a whisper, and his demeanor to that of a child caught with his hand in the cookie jar.

"Yes, sir. Three. President Liao, Chairman Tao, and General Dai Min. He said those should be enough to convince you that he has the document and has read it. Sir, he also mentioned that you haven't told the Trustees that you've lost that USB drive—"

"Stop!" Lang's hand was shaking almost uncontrollably when he picked the glass of whiskey up. He took a big gulp and nearly choked on it.

"It is true then," said Lin. "And you've pulled us into this mess with you."

Lang nodded and mumbled, "I'm... I don't..."

"We're as good as dead, I—"

"Shut up, woman! I'm trying to think." Lang turned to Dong. "Did he tell you what's in the document?"

"No, sir. Only that if he were to make it public, you'll be executed for treason, and everyone associated with you will be thrown in jail."

"What does he want?"

"He said he wants to talk to you, sir."

"And if I don't?"

"He didn't say, sir."

Lang nodded again, slowly. "When?"

"Tonight, sir. I'm to send him a text message, if—"

"Do it."

Dong took his cellphone out, retrieved the phone number given to him by the man the night before, and typed the word AGREED in the text box and sent it.

Chapter Ten

A GENERAL CHAT

Beijing, China

When the doorbell chimed at 8:30 p.m., three very anxious people in the living room were startled and almost jumped out of their chairs. They had been waiting for it for more than an hour.

Lin went to answer the door.

When the same man with the scary big black dog from the night before walked into the room, Dong felt cold shivers running up and down his spine.

Lang said nothing. He remained seated, held onto the empty whiskey glass, and stared at the man and the dog, not in surprise but like a man who had come to the end of his struggle and was left with one final choice: death or surrender. Clearly, General Lang had chosen the latter; there was a flicker of hope in his eyes.

Even so, Lang tried to feign superiority. "So, you're the man who has the audacity to try and blackmail a three-star

General of the People's Liberation Army? Who the hell do you think you are?"

Digger never took kindly to anyone being rude to the members of his pack. He walked right in front of Lang, about two steps away, sat down, and growled softly. The hair on his back stood on end.

Lang opened his mouth and started to say something. Digger snarled with exposed fangs, and the general's mouth slammed shut mid-sentence.

"General Lang, cut the crap," said Rex. "You're a dead man walking, and you know it. I'm here to offer you an opportunity to stay alive. So, what's it going to be?"

Lang's bravado was gone. He stared at the floor, refusing to meet Rex's eyes, and whispered, "Life, of course, unless the price is too high to make that choice."

Rex had to suppress a grin. He had been right about Lang being ready for recruitment. "I suspect you know why I'm here. So, do you want Lin and Dong here when we talk or not?"

Lang must have thought about it before Rex's arrival. "They stay."

Rex suppressed another grin. Lang wanted Lin and Dong to be in the same boat as he was. Their mere presence would make them traitors just like him—conspirators at the very least. The three of them would have the same motivation to keep their mouths shut—precisely what Rex wanted.

"Good, let's get started." Rex took his satphone out, put it on the coffee table, and switched it off. It was a gesture of goodwill. No recordings.

Lang did the same, so did Dong and Lin a few seconds later. In accordance with Rex's instructions, Dong had installed the GPS tracking app on Lang's phone that morning when he did the daily security check of the general's office, phones, and computer. Since then, the Peregrine IT team tracked and logged the general's every move as they'd been doing with Dong since the night before.

Rex didn't tell them that although his phone looked as if it was switched off, it was not. It was suppressing all cellphone signals in the house broadcasting on the Chinese cellular network frequencies. He also thought it unnecessary for them to know that Catia and three of Jethro Matz's bodyguards were outside, watching the house. The guards had been watching the house since the night before when Rex gave them the address. Two different guards had been following Dong since then as well.

Furthermore, they also had no need to know that he was fitted with a Molar Mic, which enabled Catia to hear everything he said and vice versa. The Molar Mic is the latest communications device for covert operators. Developed by Sonitus Technologies, the device consists of a mouthpiece equipped with a waterproof microphone, custom-built to fit the teeth of the operator. Once in place, the wearer can speak normally. The mouthpiece translates incoming audio into vibrations on the teeth that travel through the bones in the jaw and skull to the inner ear, which convert them into sounds, making it feel as if the sounds are coming from within the person's own head.

On Digger's collar was an array of very powerful miniature microphones, disguised as metal studs which would pick up any sound within a five-yard range and stream it to the base station held by Catia, from where it was relayed to a CIA communications satellite which passed it on to the Peregrine team's ops room in Langley.

All these devices were operating on frequencies not blocked by Rex's mobile phone.

"Before we continue, I want to establish your bona fides," Lang insisted.

"No problem, but let's just clarify one matter first."

"What?"

"I'm sure *you* know who I work for, but do they?" Rex pointed at Lin and Dong.

They were shaking their heads.

"I work for the CIA." Lin and Dong looked shocked. That was Rex's intention. One more door of escape had closed for them now that they knew they were collaborating with the enemy.

"Okay, with that out of the way, let's establish my bona fides as you suggested," said Rex with a smile of confidence.

"Have you read the document on the memory stick?" Lang started.

"Yes, I have."

"Who wrote the document?"

"Thirteen men, including you, who call themselves the Trustees."

"Name them."

Rex rambled the names off without using his fingers and noticed that Lang blinked a few times when he mentioned Zhì Zhě, the Wise Man.

"Give me an overview of what's in the document."

Rex had an eidetic memory. He would've been able to quote large parts of the document verbatim if asked to do so. He gave Lang the ten-minute outline.

Lang nodded. "I'm convinced that you've indeed got the document in your possession."

Rex smiled as if to say, "I wouldn't be here if I didn't."

"Final question. What happened to Sun Yan and his family?"

Rex didn't blink an eye when he told the story; he even

managed to fix a sad look on his face. "I don't know all the details. We know somehow they crossed over the border into Afghanistan in the area known as the Wakhan Corridor Nature Refuge. There they ran into a group of Taliban fighters and were killed. All three of them.

"A platoon of US Marines happened to be in the area at the time, heard the shots, and went to investigate. The Taliban fled when the Marines appeared. Unfortunately, they were too late; Sun Yan, his wife, and his daughter were dead. The Marines searched the bodies and backpacks for IDs and found the red USB flash drive, laptop, and mobile phones."

Lang was staring at Rex as if he was one of his underlings trying to tell him a tall tale. But after a while, the scrutiny stopped, and he nodded. "Let's get on with it."

People that betray their countries are usually motivated by one or more of the following: Fear. Greed. Disillusionment. Lang was not disillusioned. He was a patriot. He loved his country and the Communist Party. He wanted to see the world under the Chinese flag. But in his current situation, he was willing to forsake loyalty because of his fear of death and his insatiable greed for money and power.

Lang wanted to get out of the country immediately. In exchange for all the information in his head, on his laptop, in his safe, and under his control, he wanted fifty million US dollars, US citizenship, new identities for him and Lin, and protection under the FBI's witness protection program. He made no mention of his wife, daughter, and husband, neither of his only grandchild nor Dong.

It took Rex the better part of an hour and a lot more diplomatic skills than he ever thought he was capable of to get Lang to understand that the CIA had no intent to meet all his demands.

Lang told him that fifty million was an insignificant amount to pay to prevent a war. Of course, he was right; it was inarguable. But the issue was that the war could only be prevented if Lang stayed in China and spied for as long as was required or until he was caught or extracted, whichever occurred first. He would be of little use if he were anywhere but in China.

In the end, Rex had to become a bit more persuasive to get Lang to see things the CIA way. Which was that he would remain in China, in his current position, from where he would feed information to his handler and help the CIA break up the evil brotherhood known as the Trustees.

Lin served food and drink as the meeting continued. Every now and then, harsh words were exchanged, but Rex would not be intimidated. He told Lang the only offer on the table was what he suggested—non-negotiable.

Lang's biggest fear was that the other Trustees would find out about his betrayal. But in the end, it was Lin and Dong who helped Lang to change his mind and agree to Rex's proposal, which included working with the CIA to undermine and destroy the Trustees. In exchange for which the CIA would extract him, and whomever else might need to be extracted, when necessary. New IDs would be supplied, they would be placed in the witness protection program, provided with modest housing and a generous monthly allowance.

With that agreement in place, Rex was able to start prodding Lang for the first tranche of information.

Lang told Rex about the Trustees' meeting the previous night and the decision to kick off the Taiwan operation in three weeks with a string of assassinations of members of the Chinese Nationalist Party (Kuomintang), the opposition party. This operation had been described in the MK Plan, but no dates had been set.

The general spoke at length about the wheeling and dealing behind the scenes to get Liao elected president. He told him about the establishment of the Trustees because Liao was a weak man who couldn't be relied upon to make crucial decisions on his own. Of course, Lang stopped short of saying that they had deliberately chosen a weak man who they could manipulate.

The skepticism about President Li Lingxin's fatal heart attack was also removed when Lang told Rex that Li committed suicide by shooting himself in the head. While Lang was talking, Rex picked up some telltales that the general was not entirely honest in his recount of the events. Rex immediately thought maybe Li was killed by one of the marshals, and Lang attempted to hide it. He made a mental bookmark and left it at that.

Lang told Rex about the dire economic straits that Liao kept warning them about at each Trustee meeting. But the Trustees had decided that the answer to the country's fiscal woes was to control the world.

He also divulged to Rex the details of all the dirty laundry of his fellow Trustees. For instance, General Jin Ping had an illegal but very lucrative money-laundering scheme going. Tao Huan had his eyes on the presidency and was looking for an opportunity to push Liao out.

"Who is Zhì Zhě, the Wise Man?"

"I've met him only once. He was introduced to me as Zhì Zhě. He's a *very* old man. He doesn't attend our meetings; he works remotely and only reviews and comments on our plans. I don't know his real name. Liao knows who he is. He insisted that we bring this Zhì Zhě onboard as an external advisor."

It was clear Lang had expected the question. And Digger's soft growl told Rex that Lang was lying. But he decided to let it go for now. There was a lot of information to process and more urgent matters to attend to than finding out who Zhì Zhě was right now. Besides, he didn't want to ruin the rapport he'd managed to build with Lang over the past few hours.

The last part of the meeting was spent setting up their communications system. Apart from electronic methods, it included old-fashioned dead-letter boxes, brush passes, codenames, passcodes, and such. Finally, they discussed extraction plans in case it became necessary to get them out of China in a hurry.

At the crack of dawn, the meeting finally ended.

In the Peregrine operations room in Langley, the Cold War veterans, Martin, John, Christelle, and Ollie, had been following the meeting in real-time just like they did the night before when Rex had recruited Dong. They were impressed with Rex's understanding of the spycraft of yesteryear. John and Ollie had recruited a few spies in their Cold War days, and all of them had been handlers of spies. But none of them had ever experienced or heard of a recruitment quite like the recruitment of Deep Mantis, the computer-generated codename for General Lang Jianhong.

Chapter Eleven

SUPERDOLLARS

Matz Island, Hong Kong

Late afternoon on the same day as the recruitment of General Lang, Rex, Catia, and Digger arrived in Hong Kong for a meeting on Matz Island. On the agenda was the recruitment of General Lang, General Jin Ping's illicit money-making scheme, and Taiwan.

Josh and Marissa were already on the way to Taipei, Taiwan's capital, as the forward team for the yet-unplanned mission to prevent the assassination of opposition party members.

As usual, Jethro and company were the same warm-hearted hosts they'd always been when their friends came to visit.

Shortly after arriving, they were in Jethro's study listening to the Daltons' account of what had transpired in Beijing over the past few days. Yaron had dialed in from Tel Aviv via a secured satellite video link, and so had Martin, John, Ollie, and Christelle from Langley. Digger and

Cupcake also attended, but they didn't have anything to contribute, probably because they were too busy with more important matters, trying to get the treats stuffed into their kongs.

After the Beijing mission had been reported on, they moved on to the matter of General Jin Ping.

The four in Langley, having had 'ringside seats' during Lang's recruitment, already knew about Jin's money laundering activities, but the others in the meeting had to be brought up to speed.

Rex told them, "Lang became aware of Jin's unlawful money-making scheme a year or so ago when the two of them got spectacularly drunk one night.

"Apparently, Jin befriended a general from the North Korean military a few years ago, and the two of them went into business together. The North Korean general has access to government-controlled printing presses producing truckloads of counterfeit US one-hundred-dollar bills.

"The Korean guy supplies the forged bills to Jin. He launders it, pays his partner thirty percent, pays another twenty percent to his laundry workers. Jin pockets between two and four million real US dollars per year after expenses. Not too shabby for a PLA general, I suppose."

"Not at all," said Jethro.

"How good are the North Koreans at this forgery?" Tamara asked.

"The best there is," said Martin. "The North Koreans have been doing three things that have been hacking us off for years. Mistreating their citizens, building nuclear weapons, and counterfeiting our money. Their forgeries are so good most banks can't detect the difference. You need a team of experts to identify what is called a superdollar or supernote. They have been in circulation since the 1980s.

"The thing is, although all our paper bills, one, two, five, ten, twenty, fifty, and one hundred, look different, they are all the same size and shape. So, the criminals collect real one-dollar bills, wash or bleach them or whatever, and reprint them as one-hundred-dollar bills. That way, they don't have to worry about the intricate composition of the paper, only the design.

"In 2013, the US designed a new one-hundred-dollar bill intended to prevent counterfeiting; it incorporated a security ribbon, color-shifting numerals and drawings, and microprinting. But a few years later, the North Koreans found a cure for that problem and were back in business."

"The North Korean money is next to worthless outside the country. Due to the sanctions, they can't buy or sell much on the international markets. So they created the superdollar and use that to buy what they want or bribe whoever can be bribed. They're putting the notes into circulation through criminal groups, drug traffickers, casinos, diplomats, covert operations, and suchlike."

"How many of these notes are in circulation?" asked Yaron.

"It's estimated that at least forty-five million US dollars in circulation at any given time are North Korean superdollars. But who knows if we can't even detect the difference between the fakes and the real ones? There are about one-point-two-trillion US dollars in cash floating around the globe. The Department of Treasury estimates about seventy million dollars of counterfeit bills, approximately one counterfeit note for every ten thousand real notes. But they were quick to add it could actually be much more than that, maybe around two-hundred million counterfeits which equate to one in four thousand notes."

There was a protracted silence as everyone processed the enormity of what Martin just told them.

"Do you know how Jin launders the money?" asked Tamara.

"Lang suspects one of the methods is through the casinos of Macau," said Rex.

"I'll not be surprised," said David. "In these parts of the world, Macau is the prime destination of money-launderers. And Beijing has been cracking down on the money-laundering activities in Macau the past few years. It's been hurting their economy. And that's part of their motivation to abolish the One Country Two Systems dogma for both Macau and Hong Kong."

One Country Two Systems is the PRC's policy of Hong Kong and Macau's governance since they became Special Administrative Regions of China in 1997 and 1999, respectively. It meant that there would be only one China. However, these regions would retain their own economic and administrative systems while the rest of mainland China remained under the communist rules of the PRC. Hong Kong and Macau had control over their own governmental system, legal, economic, and financial affairs, including trade relations with foreign countries independent from those of the mainland.

The problem China has with Macau is money laundering. Wealthy people from the mainland are taking their money out of China by making withdrawals from their bank accounts with credit and debit cards that appear to be domestic transactions. Thereby they avoid China's strict limits on how much money people could move across its borders. Instead, the money is laundered at the casinos, from where they take it to other places in the world.

One case in point was when the Chinese police busted

an underground money-smuggling ring laundering more than USD \$4.4 billion through the casinos of Macau. The case was a high-profile example of Beijing's crackdown on attempts to dodge its capital controls that destabilized the Chinese economy.

Jethro knew two high-ranking officials in the Macau government on a personal basis; the Secretary for Economy and Finance and the Commissioner Against Corruption. David knew several of the tycoons who owned casinos in Macau; he was their financial advisor. Therefore, Jethro and David agreed to put their feelers out to their contacts to try and find more information about the crooked PLA general, Jin Ping.

It was time to talk about Taiwan.

Chapter Twelve

A COMPLICATED POLITICAL SCENE

Taipei, Taiwan

The political scene in Taiwan is complicated. The country's uncertain and paradoxical international political status and one hundred and ninety-four registered political parties for 23.57 million people are only two contributing factors. Political parties are not categorized as right or left on the traditional basis of economic or social policies. Instead, they are differentiated by those who want Taiwan to unite with China (but not under communist rule) and those who strived for an independent, internationally recognized Taiwan.

Before Taiwan became diplomatically isolated during the 1970s and 1980s, the Kuomintang (KMT), aka the Nationalist Party of China, was the dominant party. Their main goal was to regain control of the mainland and oust the Communist Party by force if necessary. However, over the years, the KMT has moderated its stance. It now favors a China-friendly policy and support for eventual unification with the mainland. The only conditions are mutual under-standing and China's democratization. They reject the proposal of 'One country, two systems' proposed by the PRC. And they are quick to point to the unrest in Hong Kong, where China's one country, two systems approach is supposed to be working so well. To ease tensions with the PRC, sidestep difficult political controversy, and normalize the cross-strait relation, the KMT has adopted the Three Noes policy: no unification, no independence, and no use of military force.

In short, the KMT is anti-separatist, the Democratic Progressive Party (DPP) is pro-separatist.

The pro-independence coalition led by the DPP domi-nates the national parliament. National representation includes the President, the Vice President, and the seats in the Legislative Yuan, where 65 representatives are from the pro-independence group and 43 from the pro-unification group. However, on the local government level, the numbers are reversed. Only 6 of the 22 mayors, magis-trates, and other executive positions are filled by pro-inde-pendence representatives, while 15 are pro-unification. Of the local council seats across the 6 special municipalities, 3 cities, and 13 counties, 394 are pro-unification, while only 254 representatives are pro-independence.

This anomaly is attributed to the influence of organized crime groups in Taiwan who are almost without exception supporting the KMT. The term 'black gold' (*hēi jīn*) is often used in the Taiwanese media when reporting about political corruption and getting money (the gold) by means of dark, secretive, and corrupt (the black) methods. It is often referred to as the iron triangle of organized crime, business, and politics.

In its early years, while still governing mainland China,

the KMT, in its efforts to consolidate power in war-torn post-imperial China, relied heavily on the assistance of organized crime groups when concessions were made to crime bosses in exchange for their support. It's a well-known fact that General Chiang Kai-shek had close ties with these crime groups in Shanghai, and many of them followed him when he fled to Taiwan during the Chinese Civil War.

The KMT's relationship with these organized crime organizations persists to this day. Over the years, many of the 'big brothers,' as the leaders of organized crime groups are called, became influential figures in Taiwan's economic and political arenas. Furthermore, these organizations are closely connected with crime groups in mainland China. The PRC, however, while clamping down on organized crime in mainland China, has been supporting its Taiwanese counterparts as part of their efforts to undermine the government of Taiwan. After all, the gangs in Taiwan supported the KMT, who wanted reunification with China. But, of course, they would never mention that the KMT staunchly opposes communism.

Across the Taiwan Strait, in Taipei, the DPP government had also been clamping down on crime groups but were nowhere near as effective as the PRC. They had to deal with three major groups, of which the United Bamboo Gang (UBG) was the largest and had the most members ingrained in Taiwan's politics and economy. UBG members considered themselves patriotic businessmen, not criminals. They have close links with military intelligence and security agencies. Yet, at the same time, they participate in illegal activities such as debt collection, loan sharking, gambling dens, hostess clubs, international drug smuggling, and human trafficking.

But the PRC government didn't execute or imprison all

the gang members in mainland China. In secret, they kept a select group of about two hundred ruffians on their 'books' for purposes of black operations. The kind of operations where 'wetwork' was required but without links to the PRC. They were called the Night Cobras.

It was on the Night Cobras that General Xia Wei, in charge of the execution of the MK plan, called for the Taiwan mission, codenamed Operation Prelude. Through various proxies, six of the best skilled, most cold-blooded Night Cobras were selected and briefed. The men had no idea that they were working for the PRC government. Even if they did, they wouldn't care; they were paid well.

The Trustees' plan was to conduct a false flag operation. The Night Cobras would assassinate four of the most prominent UBG leaders, as well as the leader of the KMT, the opposition party in Taiwan's parliament, and his wife. All of it would be blamed on the DPP, the ruling party, and used as an excuse by the PRC to invade Taiwan in order to protect the people originating from mainland China, the Han Chinese, who made up ninety-five percent of the population. To them, it didn't matter that the vast majority of them didn't want to be part of the PRC and rejected communism outright.

Chapter Thirteen

THE RUN-UP TO THE PRELUDE

Taipei, Taiwan

Within twenty-four hours of learning from Deep Mantis (General Lang) about the Trustees' plan to kick off the Taiwan mission, Lauren Woods, the Secretary of State, and Howard Lawrence, Director of the CIA, were dispatched by the President of the United States, on an incognito trip to Taipei for a top-secret meeting with the President of Taiwan.

The President of Taiwan was not surprised or shocked when she heard about the plan. When it came to the under-handed tactics of the PRC to intimidate and terrorize her country, there was not much she'd put past them. Regardless, she was deeply concerned. It was the first time that the threats coming from across the strait for so long were going to end in the actual invasion of her country.

Her dilemma was that she could not entrust the prevention thereof to her own security agencies. They'd been infiltrated by members of the UBG and others loyal to the

KMT. And although the PRC's intended actions were aimed against her political foes, she had no choice but to do everything within her power to protect them. After all, she believed in democracy. They'd probably never know she'd done so, neither would her own cabinet or security agencies.

The only option was to ask the US to handle it on behalf of Taiwan. But the US had its own dilemma. They couldn't do it in any official capacity; it would create a major international crisis. Any US military presence in Taiwan would be regarded as an act of aggression against China. The PRC leadership had made that clear on several occasions.

The president and his CWC knew they were walking a tightrope. Sending in US Special Forces was considered, but if the operation went south and it came to light that the US was involved, it would be a disaster. CRC had no direct links to the US government—in other words, they were deniable. But that was only half of their problem. The fact was China could not be allowed to invade Taiwan. So, they needed a backup plan if the CRC operation failed. But if they put the US military on alert, everyone would want to know why. Telling them the truth would give China an excuse to mobilize their military as well. It would quickly destroy an already tense and fragile relationship and deteriorate to the point of no return, with the US and China pointing nuclear weapons at each other.

But then, knowing about the looming attack on Taiwan and not taking any preventative actions would be tantamount to treason.

The CWC debated the option of confronting President Liao with the intelligence and read him the riot act. That might stop the PRC from attacking Taiwan, but China would then know the US had a copy of the MK Plan, and moles were operating in their midst.

Rex Dalton and his team had to do it.

The President of Taiwan was very specific about the outcome she desired. No comeback to her government, and in the words of Lawrence of Arabia, "No prisoners!"

The CWC decided as a backup, the president should order the US Navy stationed in Guam to go to full battle readiness level. The reason? Information had been received that North Korea was about to start testing nuclear-tipped long-range missiles, and some of them might be heading for Guam. The US Navy would also commence exercises mimicking a response to a surprise attack on the US fleet in the South China Sea. And finally, Submarine Squadron 15 (also known as SUBRON 15), a squadron of submarines based at Naval Base Guam consisting of the Los Angeles-class submarines USS Oklahoma City, Chicago, Key West, and Topeka, would deploy to the Taiwan Strait immediately.

In the run-up to Operation Prelude d-day, the PRC was doing their damndest to create the 'right' political climate and succeeded to a large degree as they increased the aggressive rhetoric about the renegade province that had to be brought in line. They also increased the number of PLA Navy vessels in the Strait of Taiwan and started buzzing Taiwan's Navy ships with their fighter planes not only to intimidate the Taiwanese but to also evaluate their response times and tactics.

Through the PRC's state-controlled social and traditional media, they upped the ante with increasing demands that the time had come to settle the ongoing Taiwan dispute for the good of the people of Taiwan. According to them, they had been living in the hope of being reunited with their brothers and sisters in mainland China for far too long.

The Peregrine team was monitoring the developments closely. Rex and his usual team, plus two experienced CRC operators, Connor Burns and Sam Price, were in Taipei monitoring things on the ground. According to Lang, the date for the first assassinations was ten days away. The problem was Lang didn't know exactly how it was going to happen. Those were operational details which only General Xia Wei, in charge of the execution of the MK plan, knew. And if Lang were to start meddling in operational matters, it would raise eyebrows, possibly compromising him.

All Rex and his team could do were to keep a close watch on their charges, like bodyguards, except that their protectees could not know about it. Not an ideal situation but the best they could do under the circumstances. However, that was about to change for the better when John called Rex to an urgent video conference.

Chapter Fourteen

A GENERAL ANALYSIS

International video call

General Jin Ping was a short, skinny, bald, and bespectacled man with an air about him that didn't quite fit his physique. Nevertheless, he carried himself as if the world owed him a debt of gratitude. For what exactly he was due this gratitude, no one but he knew. Maybe he felt that being in charge of the cyberwarfare division of the PLA set him apart from everyone else. After all, who else could claim that they were in charge of the cyber-espionage unit that penetrated the inner sanctum of the United States Office of Personnel Management (OPM) to harvest the names of eighteen million people working for the US government? The names included military and security agencies, in the past and present, even those who applied to work for them? Or who else would have hundreds of millions of fake social media accounts with which they could manipulate public opinion, even election outcomes? Or who else could claim to be stealing US trade secrets, billions of dollars worth every year, and get away with it?

His downfall would be his pompous arrogance and the fact that he had very few unspoken thoughts, especially when he had a few drinks and an audience.

Within a few days after the meeting with Rex et al. on Matz Island, information about the life of General Jin started flowing in. The Matzs' and David Sarlin's vast network of connections among the high-flyers of Beijing and Macau knew a lot about Jin and were happy to share the information. Another source of information was Flat Arrow, who had worked under General Jin before he defected to the US. Thus, the Peregrine analysts led by Stacie Barrett were able to create a comprehensive and accurate profile of Jin.

Stacie was a meticulous worker, near anal-retentive, with an uncanny ability to see connections between seemingly unrelated pieces of information to reveal the whole picture and a remarkable ability to recollect. Her mannerisms had earned her the nickname M1 or Abrams, a reference to the US M1 Abrams battle tank. She didn't possess a single bone of political correctness in her body, but she got results, and her team members loved her.

Her nickname had nothing to do with her looks—she was tall, in good shape, with curly dark brown hair and sparkling brown eyes—she was quite attractive. She never married; her work, two cats, a flower garden, and nature photography kept her contented.

When she was ready with her assessment, she requested a meeting to apprise everyone who had a need to know. Rex, Catia, and Digger were dialed in from their hotel room in Taipei via a secured satellite video link. With Stacie in the secured meeting room in Langley were John, Christelle,

Cupcake, and Ollie. Yaron had dialed in from Tel Aviv, and Jethro, Tamara, and David from Matz Island. Josh and Marissa were out on a reconnaissance trip to check out the locations of the planned assassinations by the Night Cobras.

"Our general seems to be one haughty son-of-a-bitch," Stacie started after being introduced to those who had never met her. Although John had given them a heads-up about Stacie's straight-shooting style prior to the meeting, their smiles said they were still somewhat amused by that opening statement.

"Apart from Jin's infatuation with himself, his own voice, and his own ideas, he also likes to conquer younger women, totally out of his league, particularly those that don't find him as sexy and charming as he believes he is. It's a challenge to which he never says no.

"He says he's a happily married man, which, according to him, doesn't mean he wouldn't cheat on his wife; he does, often. He says she knows about it. But he has this convoluted theory that she adores him notwithstanding. Because, says he, despite his infidelity, she continues to be married to him. She knows that he has many women, but she knows she remains his number one choice, and for that, she apparently adores him."

"Son-of-a-bitch indeed," mumbled Christelle, which got nods and grins from the others.

"So, whoever's going to try and recruit Don Juan's ass would do well to remember that he's a man who likes to have his ego stroked. The more, the better. And if you're going to use a honeytrap, make sure she understands he will be bewitched by any beautiful woman who wants nothing to do with him on the first approach. He would drop everything, including his guard, and take up the challenge.

"He visits Macau at least once a month, sometimes

twice. Usually over weekends. We already know or strongly suspect that's where he launders the counterfeit money. As to how he does it, we believe he uses the young women that he seduces. Only God knows how he manages to do it with looks and a repulsive ego such as his, but then, it's not rhino horn; it's money that's the most powerful aphrodisiac known to mankind.

"Finally, our IT team was able to get a good look at Jin's calendar. He's due back in Macau this weekend, three days hence."

When Stacie finished her presentation, John looked at Rex and said, "Son, you look like you need a bit of time off. I prescribe a weekend in Macau with the missus."

Rex looked at Catia. She was smiling. "I've already booked our flights."

"C'mon, I don't believe that. When?"

"While Stacie was talking." She showed him the booking confirmations on her laptop screen.

"Attagirl," said John.

Chapter Fifteen

THE HOOK

The Venetian, Macau Island

Visitors from mainland China to Macau require a two-way permit. General Jin Ping had such a permit, but the name on it was Hou Jingyi, a businessman from Beijing. The photo inside was of a skinny man with a full head of slightly graying dark hair and no eyeglasses. The disguise made him look at least a decade younger than his actual fifty-six. He cleared customs at Macau International Airport a little after 6:00 p.m. on Friday and took a taxi to the Venetian Macau resort hotel, home to the world's biggest casino. He had a reservation for one of the 753 square feet Royale deluxe suites.

The owner of the Venetian Macau was a very good friend of David Sarlin. Understandably, he was more than a little irate when he learned about General Jin's money laundering activities at his casinos over the past few years. He ordered his head of security to cooperate fully with Rex's team.

By 7:15 p.m., dressed in a dark suit and open-neck white shirt, carrying a small briefcase, Jin entered the casino area. The impossibly large halls and extravagant decorations never ceased to amaze him. But he didn't head for the gambling tables; he walked the floors in search of prey. The gambling would come later.

Half an hour of reconnaissance produced his first target; she was impossible to miss. The young woman, obviously of European descent, had shoulder-length waves of stunning auburn hair, flawless creamy skin, a scattering of light freckles across her nose. She was breathtakingly beautiful. She sat alone at a table in the bar area, a glass of red wine in front of her, flipping her gaze between her phone, her watch, and the door as if she was expecting someone.

Jin slowed down when he saw her, changed direction, and passed close by her table; he couldn't take his eyes off her. But she didn't make eye contact—she didn't even notice him. Getting closer, Jin noticed what he thought to be a worried, maybe even sad, look on her face. He kept walking and found himself a table from where he could keep an eye on her and ordered a glass of red wine.

About fifteen minutes or so later, the woman had taken only two sips of her wine, and she looked as if she was about to start crying. It was the moment Jin had been waiting for. He picked up his glass of red wine and walked over to her table.

He addressed her in English. "Excuse me, ma'am, I couldn't help but notice that you look very upset. Care if I join you for a drink? I see we both like red wine."

The woman looked up and met his eyes for the first time. Her eyes were aquamarine blue, like the Mediterranean—stunning.

"It's a free country; you can sit wherever you like. But

I'm not looking for company." Her eyes were swimming in tears.

"I take it you've been stood up by someone?"

She nodded.

"Same as I. Maybe we could cheer each other up while we're waiting for our dates? I'm Hou Jingyi."

She turned her eyes to him slowly. "Marina."

"You've got an accent, Marina. Where are you from?"

"Italy."

"Where in Italy?"

She ignored him while she did the looking at her watch-cellphone-door routine again, and with her eyes still fixed on the door, she said, "Rome."

"I've never been to Rome. I hear it's a wonderful city. What do you do for a living?"

"Too many questions, Jingyi; I told you I'm not in the mood to talk. Definitely not to strangers."

"We're not strangers; you know my name, I know yours..."

"Computer programmer," she replied while looking at her watch, cellphone, and the door again. She sighed loudly as in defeat and said, "The bastard is not coming. I might as well drink." She downed the rest of her wine in two big gulps.

"Another?"

She nodded.

Jin waved the waiter over and ordered two glasses of the same.

When the drinks arrived, she took a sip, looked at Jin, and said, "So, what do *you* do for a living?"

About two hours later, Jin had finished his sixth glass of red wine, and he was too intoxicated to notice that the woman was still as sober as when he saw her the first time.

He was unaware that the waiter had been serving her red grape juice all this time. Neither did he know that she had a Molar Mic fitted in the back of her mouth, enabling her to communicate with her husband, Rex Dalton. The latter was in an office upstairs watching them on a bank of CCTV screens.

Jin saw the big blond man and his very attractive dark-haired companion a few tables away but didn't pay them any further attention. He had no way of knowing that they were American and that they were best friends of the woman he was trying to seduce.

Jin was doing what he loved most, talking about himself.

Catia listened and pretended to enjoy his company; it wasn't easy—Jin was every bit as egocentric and vile as Stacie said. But it was for a good cause, so she endured.

He was not too inebriated to recognize that she'd warmed up to him over the past two hours. She laughed at his jokes and apparently didn't stress anymore about her date being a no-show. He believed his charms were working. It was time to make his next move—flash the money. "I had been looking forward to this evening to hit the blackjack tables. I guess you had the same idea?"

"Yes, I'm only here for one night. When will I ever get the chance to gamble in the biggest casino in the world again? Ah well, I guess it's not meant to be. In any case, that idiot is history."

"I say stuff our dates. Let's go and try our luck on the blackjack tables?"

"Best idea I've heard all night." She downed her drink and stood. "Let's do it."

It was only when she stood next to him that Jin realized for the first time how much taller she was than him, a good six inches. He was going to be the envy of every man at the gambling tables tonight.

Jin picked the briefcase up and led the way to the cashier's desk, where he put it on the counter and opened it, making sure Marina could see the contents—stacks of US one-hundred-dollar bills. He took one stack out, ten thousand US dollars, and exchanged it for chips. Half of which he gave to Marina. "Let's take them to the cleaners."

She protested, but he persuaded her to accept. After all, that's the amount he was going to give to his date. Marina eventually agreed but on the condition that she would give back whatever was left at the end of the night, including winnings, if any.

An hour later, when a man in a black suit, white shirt, and red bowtie whispered into Jin's ear, Catia was a thousand dollars up, and Jin was two thousand down.

He was irritated about the interruption. But he nodded to the man and turned to Catia. "Apologies, management wants to see me. I think they want to extend me a line of credit. I'll be back soon. In the meantime, take my chips and see if you can recover my losses; you seem to be in luck at the moment."

She smiled and said, "I'll do my best. Don't be long. The night is still young."

Jin had a satisfied smirk on his face as he left—like a man who *knew* a stunning woman was going to share his bed tonight.

Neither Jin nor any of the other patrons at the table heard when Catia whispered behind her hand, "He's on his way, Rex. That briefcase is stuffed to the brim with US dollars."

Josh and Marissa were at the table next to Catia's and got the same message through their Molar Mics.

Chapter Sixteen

THE STING

The Venetian, Macau Island

The man with the red bowtie led Jin to an office door on the second floor, knocked, and waited.

A voice from behind the door shouted in Mandarin, "Enter!"

The manager opened the door, showed Jin in, closed it behind him, and left.

Behind an enormous wooden desk sat an Asian man who Jin guessed could be in his mid-thirties. He was about five-foot-eleven in height, with penetrating dark eyes, the physique of a gymnast, and a stern-looking facial expression. Next to the man stood a mean-looking big black dog, unleashed. The dog growled softly when Jin entered.

Jin knew nothing about dogs; even if he did, he could not have known that this dog was a former Australian Special Forces dog, and he was extremely intelligent. The man behind the desk, if asked, would tell Jin that this dog was the best lie detector and judge of character on the planet. Case in point, that soft growl was to let the man know that the person who had just entered the room was not to be trusted.

Jin was unsteady on his feet. The man pointed at the empty chairs in front of the desk and said, "Please have a seat, Mister Hou."

Jin immediately knew there was not going to be any credit extended to him tonight. He went on the offensive. "Who are you? What the hell is going on?"

"My name is Xu De. I'm an agent of the Commission Against Corruption—"

"Corruption! You better have a very good explanation, Xu."

Rex held his hand up to stop Jin. "There *is* a very good explanation, sir. The ten thousand dollars you exchanged earlier are counterfeit, all of them."

The Mandarin word *fēihuà* has thirty-eight possible translations into English. In this context, it meant bullshit. The Mandarin language has quite a rich vocabulary of swearwords. Rex knew a few of them but nowhere near as many as Jin was using. To Rex, it sounded as if Jin was stringing together long sentences consisting only of profanities and not repeating any of them.

Rex didn't stop Jin; he just stared at him, waiting for the storm to run out of vocabulary. It took about a minute or so before he got a word in. "Okay, I see you want to do it the hard way, general—"

"What did you call me?"

"You heard me, General Jin Ping."

"My name is Hou Jingyi. I'm a businessman from Beijing."

"No, that's not true. You're General Jin. You're in charge of Information Operations and Information

Warfare, the cyber warfare division of the PLA, and you're guilty of using counterfeit money to defraud this establishment. We know a lot more about you than you might think, general. You might as well remove the wig and contact lenses; they do nothing to hide your identity."

Jin looked as though he had been poleaxed. Adrenaline doesn't really sober a drunk person up; it only increases alertness and energy, but it certainly looked as if Jin were sober now.

It took a long while before he had collected enough composure to speak again. He kept the wig and contact lenses, though. He spoke in an unnaturally calm and measured tone that betrayed his shock. "One, seeing that you know who I am, then surely you know you can't lay a finger on me. Two, I challenge you to prove that the money I exchanged is counterfeit."

Rex raised his index finger. "One, this was a sting operation—"

"A sting operation! You ran a sting operation against a two-star PLA general? You must have a death wish."

"Well, it was a joint operation between the Commission Against Corruption, the MSS, and the American FBI—"

"FBI! How the hell, who..."

"General, you'll *have* to give me a chance to finish."

Jin ignored the request and launched into another barrage of invective but stopped abruptly and glowered at Rex. Probably because it finally dawned on him that the MSS was involved. He needed no introduction to them. The Ministry of State Security (MSS), China's intelligence, security, and secret police agency responsible for counterintelligence, foreign intelligence, and political security, had a reputation as one of the most secretive and brutal intelligence organizations in the world. Jin knew that to be accurate; he had seen them in action.

"The thing is, general, we're all fed up with the hundreds of millions worth of counterfeit money floating around, hurting our economies. So, I'm not so sure your rank is going to get you out of this mess. But I could be wrong. However, be that as it may, that's not for me to decide. I'm to place you under arrest and hand you over to the MSS and let justice take its course."

Bile was welling up in Jin's throat. He swallowed.

"Two," Rex held up a second finger, "the FBI and MSS forensic experts are in the room next door. I'll call them in to explain to you how they've determined that the money is fake."

As if on cue, there was a knock on the door. "Enter!" Rex shouted.

Josh and Marissa entered. Following them was a short man, about five foot two, fair-skinned and stern-faced. One look at him, and Jin knew that this man's lack of height should not be mistaken for inability to be lethal. He was right. This man was Jethro Matz's head of security, a former Ghurka. His name was Ramesh Ojha.

Rex said, "Ah, good of you to come. I was about to call you. This is General Jin Ping of the PLA. General, meet agent Long," Rex pointed to the short man, "he's with the MSS. And those two are agents Reynolds and Wiley; they're with the FBI."

So far, Digger had played his part brilliantly. He didn't show any signs that he knew Josh and Marissa or Ojha or that he was happy to see them. Instead, he had sat down when they came in and smiled at them. But Jin didn't know it was a smile the dog had on his face and not a sign of aggression. He swallowed again and eyed the door.

Digger must have seen or sensed it. He got up, walked to the door, sat down, and stared at Jin as if to say the famous words of Harry Callahan (Clint Eastwood) in the Dirty Harry movies, "You've got to ask yourself one question: 'Do I feel lucky?'"

Apparently, Jin didn't feel lucky; he turned his gaze back to Rex.

So far, the conversation had been in Mandarin. Josh and Marissa knew no more than three or four words in Mandarin.

Rex told Jin that the FBI agents didn't speak Mandarin, to which Jin immediately replied, "And I don't speak English."

Rex translated.

Josh said, "Great. Saves me a lot of trouble. I was going to try and have a conversation with him first and ask nicely where he got the fake money. But if he doesn't understand what I'm saying, I might as well go straight to the part where I put the drops of battery acid in his eyes and ears." Josh took a small bottle with a dropper screw-top out of his jacket pocket and placed it on the desk. Had Jin been wearing his usual glasses, he would have been able to see that it was eyedrops.

As it were, he couldn't read the label and shouted in English, "You can't do that! I'm a two-star general in the PLA. You—"

Josh hit a fist into an open palm. "*Damn*, my career counselor was right. I should've gone into English language teaching rather than join the FBI. I could've been a very rich man selling my rapid English course to Mandarin speakers."

Rex and Marissa managed not to explode in laughter.

Ojha was a serious man; he didn't even grin. But Jin was deeply humiliated and annoyed.

In English, Rex said, "General, remember this was a sting operation against you. We know all about you. We've been following you from the moment you boarded the plane in Beijing earlier today." Rex was lying, but Jin wouldn't know. "We've been listening to all your conversations, including your attempted seduction of the Italian woman, Marina. We know you're fluent in English. Stop the farce, and let's get on with it."

Jin's shoulders were slumped as he stared at the floor in silence for a long time. A defeated man. Finally, he whispered, "What can I do to get out of this mess?" He didn't even bother to ask who had betrayed him. He probably knew all too well that he had bragged at least one too many times about his very lucrative side business.

"Well, I'm not sure there is much you *can* do. In any case, as I've said, it's not within my authority to do anything but place you under arrest and hand you over to the MSS agent."

Jin sighed loud and long.

"However, I'm sure the FBI and MSS agents here will put in a good word for you if you cooperate fully with us." Rex was looking at the 'agents' with raised eyebrows.

They were nodding.

Jin started talking. He tried a few omissions and some outright lies but quickly discovered that the agents seemed to know everything; they only wanted him to tell it in his own words. Everything was being videotaped.

The final straw was when the sensational Italian woman whom, an hour or so ago, he was certain would share his bed that night, walked in without knocking and said to the man behind the desk, "Ah, there you are, darling. I've been waiting for you in the bar; you've missed all the fun." Then she turned to Jin and said, "General Jin, you won't believe what a stroke of good luck I had while you were away. I've recovered all your losses." She placed a stack of US one-hundred-dollar bills on the table. Jin didn't have to be told those were the same bills he had exchanged earlier.

That's when the last bit of Jin's resistance broke, like a dam wall already leaking like a sieve finally giving up and collapsing.

Seeing a two-star PLA general, one of the most powerful men in China, fall apart and break down in tears was not a pleasant sight. The onlookers experienced a small measure of sympathy but not for long. They reminded themselves of the immeasurable, irreparable damage this man and his cadres with their cybercrimes caused people and countries across the globe.

Hours later, Jin had not only built his own metaphorical gallows but also supplied the rope, ascended the stairs on his own, and placed the noose around his own neck. Jin had no illusions that all it would take for the man with the big black dog to pull the lever which would open the trapdoor below his feet and let him plunge to his death was to double-cross him in any manner.

Langley, Virginia, USA

Martin, John, Christelle, Ollie, and Stacie, even Cupcake, had broad smiles on their faces when the meeting with General Jin Ping came to an end. Though Cupcake's smile probably stemmed from her expectation that she would be getting another treat soon.

Martin started. "Good work, team. Bagging two PLA generals, an aide de camp, and a general's mistress in ten days is a major feat. I'm not sure even the three of you could've pulled something like this off in your heydays."

"Different enemy, different times, and different technologies," Ollie remarked. "But I have to admit this was impressive."

"Except, of course," said Stacie, "letting the scumbag keep two and a half million dollars of his ill-gotten gains. That felt like kissing Adolf Hitler on the mouth."

Everyone started laughing.

John was still chuckling. "Yeah, it goes against the grain, doesn't it? But, with these coerced recruitments, it's important not to drive the subject over the cliff of despair. One has to leave them with a glimmer of hope, like a light at the end of the tunnel. If Jin didn't have the promise that we would extract him when the time comes and the means to start a new life, he'd have only two options right now—run and hide or suicide. None of those are good for us. He loves life and money more than his country; we've given him both."

Stacie nodded. "I understand, but it doesn't make it less galling."

Ollie smiled. "Stacie, in the spy business, the boundaries of morality are sometimes blurred. If kissing Hitler is what it takes then... well... you take a deep breath, close your eyes, and imagine it's Clark Gable."

"Don't ever ask me to do it. I've got no imagination whatsoever."

Ollie laughed. "I'll keep that in mind."

Jin Ping, codenamed Dusty Wolf, was, by all accounts, a much bigger catch than Lang Jianhong. Through Jin, the Peregrine IT team now had backdoor access to all of Unit

61398's servers. Flat Arrow's access to the unit's servers was limited to only those that he and his team needed for their specific tasks, while Jin had full administrator access to all servers. It was like getting access to the entire library instead of just a few books.

In addition, Jin, because he was the most technically savvy of the Trustees, was the designated scribe at their meetings. No one else was allowed to make any recordings whatsoever. Jin recorded everything on his computer and used a speech-to-text application to convert it. At the end of each meeting, within minutes, he was able to provide each of the attendees with a flash drive containing the transcribed document. Zhì Zhě's copy was uploaded to his private server hosted in one of Unit 61398's secured server rooms, to which only Jin had access.

Equally exciting was the access they now had to the computer network of General Xia Wei's Operation MK ops center. The team supplied Jin with a trojan horse virus to propagate itself to all computers on the network. Thus, after Jin installed the virus on a network-linked computer, they could eavesdrop on all conversations in the ops center.

The first piece of life-saving information they wanted, which the IT team was already working to retrieve, was the Operation Prelude details.

D-day was only five days away.

En route to Beijing, China

On the flight to Beijing, Jin had almost all but damaged his brain trying to figure out who had betrayed him. But his ego, what was left of it, didn't permit him to admit that the real cause of his downfall was the unholy trinity; I, me, and myself.

Unquestionably, it had been the worst day of his life. He had been humiliated beyond description. He had been terrorized into becoming a traitor. And worst of it all, there was absolutely nothing he could do about it, except for suicide. But he had this thing about living... and money.

How they found out about his secret Swiss account was another maddening question. He thought Swiss banks were safe and secure. But Jin didn't know it was a fallacy. Generally speaking, Swiss banks would keep the details of their clients' secret. Unfortunately for people like Jin, that stopped as soon as security agencies, such as the CIA, FBI, MI5, MI6, and others came knocking in search of dirty money. Consequently, the CIA relieved him of a little over twenty million dollars, leaving him two and half million in the account he couldn't access unless he pleased them.

Operation Prelude. The Trustees. Shit! There were only thirteen people on this planet who knew... were supposed to know... The traitor must be one of the Trustees! But none of them knew anything about his Swiss bank account... or did they?

When his plane landed in Beijing, Jin was a changed man. He considered himself fortunate to still be a free man, and he intended to keep it that way by cooperating fully with the man with the big black dog and his associates.

Chapter Seventeen

WEEDS IN THE GARDENS

Taipei, Taiwan

The arrival of the six Night Cobras in Taiwan three days before d-day was expected and duly monitored by Rex and his team Catia, Digger, Josh, Marissa, and two more CRC operators, Connor Burns and Sam Price. Thanks to Jin Ping, they had photos and a plethora of information about every one of the gangsters.

They arrived on two different flights at the Taoyuan International Airport in Taipei. The first group of four men was tasked with the assassination of the four UBG leaders. The second group of two men was responsible for the assassination of the opposition leader and his wife. The two groups didn't know about the existence of the other.

Their passports were Taiwanese but false, supplied by UBG members working at the Ministry of Foreign Affairs. Nevertheless, none of them experienced any issues to clear customs.

They were wholly unaware that their luggage had been tagged with GPS tracking devices before they collected it. Neither did they know that their cellphones had been compromised to the Peregrine IT team in Langley before they'd even left China. Nor that within less than thirty minutes after clearing customs, the official records had been sanitized; none of them had ever been in Taiwan.

The four-man team traveled by shuttle bus to a safe house on the outskirts of Taipei. The two-man team traveled to a different safe house on the opposite side of the city via taxi.

All six of them were on high alert, looking out for watchers and followers but didn't spot any. The electronic tracking through their luggage and the GPS location software on their cellphones eliminated the need for physical observation.

At the respective safe houses, they found the fridges and shelves stocked with food. There were vehicles, weapons, observation, and surveillance equipment, communications equipment, and stashes of cash. They had the names, photos, addresses of their targets, and their schedules for the next few days. They had two and a half days to reconnoiter the sites and the targets. The four UBG leaders played mahjong once a week on a Wednesday night. That's when the hit would take place.

The opposition leader and his wife lived in a mansion not far from the second safe house. They were usually in bed by no later than 10:00 p.m. The house was fitted with an electronic alarm system connected to the local police station, but there were no guards. The hit on them would take place on the same night as the hit on the UBG leaders.

The two teams made one reconnaissance trip of the

target locations during the daytime, the day after their arrival in Taiwan, and another trip the night after. The rest of the time, they stayed out of sight, played cards, and consumed a lot of alcohol.

For Rex and his team, it would have been much easier and less risky to surprise and eliminate the six men at their respective safehouses in the days before the assassinations. But the Taiwanese president was adamant that she wanted them taken out only after they'd committed themselves to the act.

In other words, Rex's teams had to wait until the assassins turned up on the premises of their targets.

Taipei, Taiwan

The estate of the UBG crime boss proclaimed wealth; a six-bedroom mansion, swimming pool, sauna, jacuzzi, a free-standing rumpus room fully furnished with a mini kitchen, bar, pool table, and more. All of it situated on two acres of land with lush gardens, surrounded by eight-foot-high brick walls, with razor wire and security cameras on top. On the north side of the property was the main road. On the east and west sides were the neighboring estates, and on the south side, a private park accessible only by those houses bordering it. The rumpus room was the place the boss used for informal gatherings and mahjong nights.

There were no guards or dogs. The security cameras were feeding two TV screens mounted on one of the walls in the boss's study. Motion sensors had been deployed throughout the garden, which would set off an alarm inside the house when triggered. Visitors either needed the six-digit security code or request access over the intercom to get through the front gate. The vulnerability of the security setup was that it had no backup generator or batteries. But it had its own power line, separate from the rest of the property.

The four Night Cobras arrived in a dark-gray Toyota RAV 4 at 10:30 p.m. and parked under a huge tree along a deserted stretch of the boundary wall, right next to the electricity company's power distribution box, decorated with paintings of mountains. Twenty seconds later, the security system was inoperative, and so was the electronic lock to the front gate. It would now open by simply pushing it. Neither the boss nor his three guests with him around the table in the rumpus room or the house's occupants were aware that the security system had gone down.

They wore black coveralls and black ski masks. Although they knew they were taking on an undefended target, they were armed to the teeth, with weapons and ammunition usually issued to the soldiers of the Taiwan Marine corps. They had to kill the four men playing mahjong in the rumpus room, but if anyone else got in the way, they had to be put down as well.

The leader pushed the front gate open, went inside, and looked around while the others waited. A few minutes later, he hand-signaled to his teammates that the coast was clear. They slipped through the gate, joined him, and started for the rumpus room at the back of the house, next to the swimming pool.

They were oblivious to the fact that a few hundred feet above their heads hovered a small helicopter drone fitted with night-vision and thermal imaging equipment transmitting video footage to Marissa Farley's laptop screen half a mile away, where she was sitting in a dark, windowless Toyota van in communication with her husband, Josh, and Connor Burns through their Molar Mics.

The Night Cobras were also unaware that when they had disabled the security system, the electronic lock on the gate at the back of the house giving access to the private park had also stopped working. Josh and Connor entered through this gate and took up positions behind the shrubs about ten yards away from the main gate next to the driveway leading to the house.

And none of the four assassins had ever seen the movie Lawrence of Arabia.

Josh's and Connor's night-vision goggles illuminated the intruders in a liquid-green glow. And the two Glock 19 pistols pointed at them were silenced.

The gangsters walked slowly and silently, stooping behind the plants, scanning around for any signs of danger. They were no strangers to violence. They were ruthless killers, which was why they were hired for this mission. Yet, for a split second, they were surprised when the nine-millimeter bullets struck their skulls, and then they abruptly ceased to be surprised—they were dead.

Within five minutes, the four bodies were in the back of the van, the security system of the estate had been reactivated. The van was on the way to pick up two more bodies on the other side of the city.

There were only three people alive who saw what had happened at the house of the UBG boss that night, and they worked for CRC. Exactly what the presidents of Taiwan and America hoped and prayed for but didn't want to know about—not officially. Thus, half of their problems had been solved, and they didn't even know about it, not yet.

On the other side of the city, Rex, Catia, Digger, and Sam Price had been in place for the past hour at the opposition leader's house. The two Night Cobras made their appearance at 10:45 p.m. By now, the cadavers of four of their colleagues were en route to this location. But they didn't know anything about that.

A few seconds after the Night Cobras's Toyota Corolla drove past the Honda SUV with Catia inside, she steered the helicopter drone she had been directing for the past five minutes to the target house. She let it hover two hundred feet above the ground.

It was a nice three-bedroom family house in a nice neighborhood, but a hovel compared to the house of the UBG crime boss. The property had fences on the sides and back but not the front. The master bedroom was at the back of the house with a door that led out on a small porch. That's where the Night Cobras were heading.

When one had connections with the Taiwan crime bosses, there wasn't much to worry about personal safety. Even so, police patrol cars passed the house three to four times a night. And the house had an alarm system which was connected to the nearest police station.

Taking control of the alarm system was a small job for General Jin Ping's Unit 61398 hackers. After that, the alarm monitors at the police station were quiet because all the signals it received confirmed that the leader of the KMT's house was safe and secure. There was no signal that the alarm system had been off for the past half an hour.

Rex, Sam, and Digger were hiding in the garage. The KMT leader and his wife had gone to bed right on time at 10:00 p.m. According to Catia, the thermal images suggested they were asleep. She kept Rex and Sam up to date with the two assassins' progress.

The men passed the side door of the garage in a low crouch, silenced guns in hand. Like their dead colleagues, they also wore black coveralls and black ski masks and were armed with weapons and ammunition from the Taiwan Marine corps.

They never heard the garage side door open behind them; neither did they hear the two silenced shots that killed them.

Within minutes their bodies were zipped up in bags and dropped in the back of the SUV Catia drove.

Half an hour later, their bodies joined those of their four dead buddies in the back of the windowless Toyota van driven by Josh. The six bodies were transported to the Port of Taipei and loaded onto a small speedboat heading out to sea. About six miles from land, weights were tied to their feet before they were dumped into the water.

In Beijing, Unit 61398 hackers had reactivated the alarm system.

The Daltons and Farleys would fly over to Hong Kong later in the day. Connor Burns and Sam Price would take a commercial flight back to the US.

Washington, D.C. | Taipei, Taiwan

It was a little after midday in D.C. The president was coming out of a meeting with some of his security advisors. In passing, Howard Lawrence whispered something into the president's ear that brought a tiny smile to his face. Not long after that, twelve time zones away, in Taipei, the President of Taiwan, burning the midnight oil, got a text message on her personal private phone. The message was short:

ALL WEEDS ERADICATED FROM THE GARDENS.

The president let out a long sigh of relief.

Beijing, China

In the underground command and control center of Operation MK, General Xia Wei waited in vain for news that he was supposed to have received more than two hours ago. By now, the airwaves were meant to be abuzz. Images of the horrible killings should have been front and center on TV screens around the world. President Liao should have been rehearsing his speech for that night. But nothing of the sort was happening. All that could be heard from across the Strait of Taiwan was a deafening silence. By the time the sun came up over Beijing, Xia knew that his assassins were not coming home.

Since being handed the reigns of Operation Middle Kingdom, he had planned and overseen two major strategic covert military operations. Both had failed, spectacularly. First in the Strait of Malacca three months ago, now Taiwan.

His head was on the chopping block—no doubt. He would be given a chance to explain how he planned and executed the Taiwan mission. That didn't worry him; he was confident no one would fault him on his plans. What worried him, though, was how to explain to the Trustees that despite his meticulous planning, the mission had failed.

And the only explanation he could think of was that there was a mole in his camp. He was not a man who swore often, but he swore now—with venom.

After a while, he got an invitation, or rather a summons, to a Trustee meeting held at Zhongnanhai at 7:00 p.m. So he had about twelve hours to find answers.

Chapter Eighteen

REMEMBERING THE GREAT FAMINE

Zhongnanhai, Beijing, China

Over the course of the past four decades, while ascending the ladder of promotion in civil service to his current position, Mao Xinya had learned that there were two types of superiors. Those who were *genuinely* too busy to read lengthy reports and those who *thought* they were too busy to read them. The president was one of the former. That's why Mao's report consisted of a one-page executive summary, followed by a five-page explanation of the causes of the impending disaster, a half-page conclusion, and five attachments of background information ranging between four and ten pages each.

After extending courteous greetings to the president, declining the offer of tea, and settling in his appointed chair, though very uneasy, he took the president's copy of the report out of his briefcase and handed it to him.

Liao placed it on the desk in front of him and left it

there, unopened. He looked at Mao, waiting to be told what was in the report.

Mao shifted in his chair. "Mr. President, I'm afraid I'm the bearer of the worst possible news. I won't waste your time by giving you a rundown of our country's agricultural affairs. You're as familiar with them as I am."

Liao nodded. Mao was right; he knew them very well.

China has to feed 1.4 billion people, about 22 percent of the world population.

China ranked about 23rd out of 67 countries on the Food Sustainability Index alongside South Korea and the UK. However, in the agricultural sustainability category, they ranked near the bottom of the index at number 57, between Indonesia and Sudan.

The country's rapid economic growth has generated new demographic demands and environmental pressures. With the increase in annual per capita income from just $330 to $9,460 over the past two decades, consumption habits have changed, which has made the country increasingly reliant on food imports, which have grown from $14 billion to over $104 billion in just 17 years.

In 1996, the PRC government had set itself a 95% self-sufficiency target for grains such as rice, wheat, and corn, and for the most part, met the target despite the fact that grain consumption had increased from 125 million metric tons to 420 million tons in four decades. During that same period, meat consumption increased from 7 million tons to over 86 million tons. As a result, China is the largest meat and grain consumer in the world.

Attempts to boost the country's agricultural production through genetically modified (GM) crops had been met by repeated public pushback.

Efforts in 2015-16 to capitalize on Australia's available

land by attempting to purchase Australia's largest cattle business, S. Kidman and Co., comprising 2.5 percent of the total Australian land area, about the size of South Korea, was blocked by the Australian government on account of concerns about national interest.

China consumes about 36 percent of the global seafood harvest, making them the largest fish consumer in the world. But within Chinese territorial waters, years of overfishing have depleted resources to the point where there is practically no fish left in the East China Sea. Therefore, China has increased its fishing activities outside its territorial waters dramatically. They now account for more than 38 percent of the global harvest—much of it illegal, unreported, and unregulated.

Liao understood full well the importance of food security and how critical it was to the safety and well-being of any country. Fragile states are often those that are the most food insecure. China was ranked 39 out of 113 countries, below middle-income countries such as Brazil, Belarus, Argentina, Costa Rica, and Mexico.

The Chinese government has always considered grain security as the highest priority, and farmers have kept up with the increased demand for its staple crops, such as rice, wheat, and corn, achieving an almost one-to-one ratio of production and consumption.

But, although China has seven percent of the world's arable land, at only 0.21 acres of arable land per capita, it's less than half of the global per capita average. There is little room for expansion. Much of the existing arable land is very difficult to cultivate because it's mountainous, arid, or salinated. And available arable land has been shrinking due to urbanization, erosion, and pollution. The shortage of arable land is further hampered by poor regulation of bad farming practices, which has caused significant environmental damage. Widespread soil contamination has prompted the government to prohibit the farming of 8 million acres of contaminated agricultural land. The bottom line is, 22 percent of the world's population has 7 percent of the world's arable land and 6 percent of its freshwater.

Those were the statistics that flashed through Liao's mind. The reality was that China was unable to produce enough food to feed itself. Even with massive government oversight to manage food production, the country remained the largest food importer in the world.

"Mr. President," Mao continued, "I also don't have to tell you that China's food supply, especially grain, has always been a balancing act. Thus far, we've been able to produce around ninety-five percent of domestic consumption and import the balance.

"This year, however, the floods in the provinces along the middle and lower Yangtze River, all of which are major rice producers, followed by the floods in the northeastern provinces, major producers of rice and corn, have destroyed close to fourteen percent of the crops. And as you know, the outbreak of African swine fever in August 2018 wiped out half of the nation's pigs. The price of pork is still over one hundred and thirty-five percent up from what it was before the outbreak." Mao paused.

Liao leaned forward. "Xinya, why do I get the impression that was the good news?"

Mao took a deep breath and stopped himself from wiping the sweat off his forehead. "Unfortunately, Mr. President, that is true. If we had to deal only with the shortages caused by the floods and the swine flu, I wouldn't have bothered you. What I'm here to tell you is that we're facing a catastrophe of epic proportions. It will take a few more weeks to finalize our forecasts and provide you with more accurate figures, but we already know that we will have almost no grain harvest this year."

Ice-cold shivers were running down Liao's spine—famine—a hellish abyss of food insecurity and starvation.

Besieged by waves of nausea, Liao not only regretted having breakfast, but he also bitterly regretted giving in to the demands of the Trustees to become the President of the People's Republic of China in the first place. The memory of China's Great Famine from 1958-62 was still vivid in the minds of those who survived it. Liao was in his early teens back then. Yet, somehow, he managed to display outward calm. "Why?"

"A fungus, sir."

"Fungus?" the president whispered.

"Yes, sir, a new kind of fungus that our scientists have never seen before."

"When was it discovered, by whom, and what has been done about it?" Liao's voice sounded as if it originated in the Arctic.

Mao was acutely aware that he could delegate a lot of things to underlings, but responsibility was not one of them. The buck stopped with him. Professor Lei's presentation was not going to exonerate him, but it might influence the president's understanding of the origin of the problem, which Mao, even though he was an atheist, considered to be an act of God.

"Mr. President, would you please allow me to bring in Professor Lei Hai, our senior agronomist and grain specialist? He will provide you with all the scientific details. He's in the waiting room."

Liao didn't make an immediate reply. Instead, he

buzzed his secretary and told her to reschedule his appointments for the rest of the day and to make sure he was not disturbed unless someone launched a nuclear attack on China. Only then did he turn to Mao and said, "Bring him in."

Chapter Nineteen

STARING AT THE HOLE IN THE WALL

Zhongnanhai, Beijing, China

Professor Lei Hai was in his early sixties. He was a little over average height, in good physical shape, had silver-gray hair, gold wireframe glasses, and was dressed in a charcoal suit, white shirt, and light-gray tie. But the professor was stuttering so much, he was struggling to speak.

Liao came to the dazed professor's rescue. "Professor, please relax. You're not in any kind of trouble. Minister Mao spoke highly of you and assured me that you're our best scientist when it comes to grain diseases. We're reliant on your knowledge to get an understanding of the problem and to work out a plan of action. You have my word; you're in no trouble whatsoever."

Lei nodded vigorously and managed to get out a coherent, "Thank you, Mr. President."

"Now," said Liao, "please start at the beginning and tell me everything about this fungus. And I mean everything.

Even if you think it's too technical for me. I'll stop and ask you if I don't understand."

Lei nodded again, took a deep breath, opened his folder, and started talking. Within a minute, he had relaxed, and it was as if he was in a classroom lecturing his students.

"Plant diseases are caused by pathogens, in other words, bacteria, fungi, viruses, and other microorganisms. Plant diseases can cause crop failures resulting in inadequate food supplies and famine in severe cases such as this. What we're dealing with here is an unknown species of fungus belonging to the *Colletotrichum* genus. Our scientists are studying it as we speak.

"Sir, two months ago, as has been our standard operating procedure for many years, we took samples of all types of grains from our seed bank and planted them at test sites across the country. The aim was to see if there were any issues with the seeds to address them in time for the new planting season. The seeds germinated as expected, but within two weeks, the plants started to wither and die."

"And this fungus is the cause of it?"

"Yes, sir."

"How much of our seed bank is infected?"

"None of it, sir. The fungus had been dormant in the soil and decaying plant matter, even equipment, for many years. Bacteria and fungi have the ability to enter long periods of a hardy, non-replicating state, known as quiescence or dormancy. During those periods of dormancy, it is immune against treatments. When the fungus eventually becomes active, it enters the stomata, or 'air vents' of the plant and starts multiplying. In the early stages, the infection is invisible to the farmer. But when it has built up enough numbers, it switches from an unwanted parasite to a wholesale destroyer, demolishing the structural supports and cells of the plant."

"All grains, even rice?"

"Yes, sir."

"You said it comes from the soil. How much of our farmland has been infected?"

"We're still conducting soil tests, sir. We've covered about eighty percent of our grain-producing soil across the country. So far, every sample has come back positive."

"In statistical terms, that means we can safely assume all of it is infected?" whispered Liao.

Mao spoke into the silence that followed. "Yes, Mr. President, that's what we're assuming at this stage. It means there will be no grain harvest this year."

Liao was silent for a long while. "How did the soil become infected in the first place?"

"Sir, decades of bad farming practices including contamination of our water sources," replied Lei. "Practices such as monoculture, growing of one type of crop on the same land year after year. Not protecting the topsoil. Overuse of pesticides which include antibiotics and fungicides leading to the mutation of bacteria and fungi to become resistant or, as in this case, resistant and dormant. Water sources are contaminated by chemicals, antibiotics, and fungicides. More than fifteen percent of our groundwater is classified as 'Grade V'—so polluted it's unsuitable for any use."

"Can you rule out bioterrorism?" Liao asked Mao.

"No, sir. At this stage, we don't have enough information to rule out anything."

"Does any other country in the world have a similar problem?"

"Not that we're aware of, sir. But I'd imagine if other

countries have a similar problem, they'd want to keep it under wraps for strategic reasons."

Liao nodded. "And we'll have to do the same. But that doesn't solve our problem, does it?"

"No sir, it doesn't," said Mao. "We consume four hundred and forty million tons of grain per year, of which we import about twenty-six million tons. So, we have about four hundred and twenty million tons stockpiled. That will see us through this year.

"The real problem is that we have no idea how to combat this fungus as yet. We first have to find a treatment, then we have to decontaminate our arable land. It could be a costly and lengthy process that could take years."

"Doomsday," Liao whispered as he put his elbows on his desk and lowered his face into his hands. "In other words, we have enough grain for one year and no prospects of producing even a fraction of what we need for next year or the year after?"

Mao shifted uncomfortably. "Yes, Mr. President. Even if we buy every kernel of grain available on the international market, we will have only half of what we need. The total global trade volume for rice is only enough for twenty-five percent of our rice consumption."

"Our farmers will be ruined financially, and the rest of the country will have no food," Liao sighed.

The meeting lasted another two hours. The president made them both take an oath that they would not discuss the report with a living soul unless authorized by him personally.

Mao left the president's office, relieved that he hadn't been blamed for the disaster—not yet. But he knew it was still in the cards. The president was a pragmatist; he wanted to address the problem first. Assigning blame would come after.

When the door closed behind Mao and Lei, President Liao turned his swivel chair and found himself staring at the hole in the wall behind his desk. The hole had been caused by the bullet which killed his predecessor, Li Lingxin. It was a stark reminder of how the marshals resolved their problems.

He started considering his options. He knew he had to report this to the Politburo. But only after he had told the Trustees. The crop failure and resultant food shortages were inevitable. The question was how to stop it from becoming a catastrophic famine. He had little doubt that the majority of Trustees would want to use military power, and that would be a fool's errand. Going to war without food would be as good as giving the enemy permission to exterminate the Chinese people. Those who would be so unfortunate not to be killed in the war would die a slow and agonizing death in the famine.

War is what the marshals will want, but peace is what the people of China needed. And right now, as far as he knew, he was the only one who could possibly keep the peace. But how to overcome the odds? One against eleven. He still had no idea who Zhì Zhě, the Wise One, was and where he would stand on the matter.

Chapter Twenty

THREE OUT OF TEN

Zhongnanhai, Beijing, China

General Lang started the meeting right on time at 7:00 p.m. He chose his words carefully. "Comrades, please accept my apologies for the short notice. But I'm sure we all want to hear General Xia's report about Operation Prelude."

Lang looked at Xia and nodded imperceptibly.

But Liao spoke first. "General Lang, my apologies for interrupting the agenda. I'm sure we all know something went wrong last night and that General Xia no doubt has an explanation. But be that as it may, what I have to tell you is of much higher urgency and importance."

All eyes were now fixed on the president. It took him about a quarter of an hour to impart to them the gist of the meeting with the Minister of Agriculture and Rural Affairs and his lead agronomic scientist that morning.

They listened in stunned silence. But when he finished, for close to an hour, they bombarded him with questions. Lang had a hard time keeping the order.

However, Liao was ready for it and answered all of them with honesty and sincerity. He left them with no doubts in his conclusion. "Comrades, we're facing the biggest crisis in our history. The challenge we have is how to survive it." He turned his gaze to Lang as if to say, "Over to you."

As expected, a few of them refused to apply their minds to find a solution before they knew who was to blame. But Liao pointed out that assigning blame and punishing the culprits wouldn't make the famine disappear. Even if it was bioterrorism, it wouldn't make the famine go away.

"If the people are starving, there will be a rebellion that we won't be able to contain," said Admiral Deng Jie, the commander of the PLA Navy.

Liao could smell the fear in the room. The men around the table were powerful, privileged, protected. But they feared one thing more than all else—the day when the working class went berserk. Those that make up the ninety-four percent of the populace who had been suppressed into tolerant, long-suffering, ox-like humans by the privileged six percent for the past seven decades.

The Tiananmen Square protests of June 1989, known in China as the June Fourth Incident, when troops armed with assault rifles and accompanied by tanks fired at demonstrators and those trying to block the military's advance into Tiananmen Square happened a little over thirty years ago but was still well-remembered. More than ten thousand died. But what the Trustees were looking at now would make Tiananmen Square look like a football match between fierce rivals.

"Comrades, the crop failure we cannot prevent," said Liao. "The food shortage we can—"

"How?" Interjected General Dai Min, the man in charge of China's nuclear arsenal.

"We ask the rest of the world to sell to us what we need—"

"Didn't you tell us just ten minutes ago if we buy everything available on the market, we'll still be fifty percent short?" Dai asked.

"I did, General, but that refers only to grain, not other foodstuffs. Every year enough food is produced on the planet to feed ten billion people, one and a half times the global population."

"The moment we attempt to do that, they'll know we're in trouble, and they'll use it against us," said Dai.

"General, there's no way we can hide it from them. Their spy satellites will soon see that we're not planting this year. We'll *have* to negotiate, and we'll *have* to make concessions—"

"To whom? America? The EU? Our neighbors?" Dai snapped.

"Any country that will sell us the food we need to survive."

"Never!" Roared General Wan Huang of the Air Force. "No concessions! We take what we need from—"

Lang interrupted and managed to calm Wan down. Then, he looked at Liao and asked, "What type of concessions do you have in mind, Mr. President?"

Liao blinked in surprise. Lang had never addressed him by his title before. He'd always used his first name—in a condescending manner most of the time. But Liao didn't have time to wonder about it. "We won't know until we start negotiating. But keep in mind we have been stockpiling gold with the goal of acquiring enough to back the Chinese yuan to become the new international monetary system. We have the sixth-largest cache of gold bullion in the world. But we might have to use that now to buy food. In my opinion, that would be a small concession given the alternative."

Only Lang, Jin, and Deng nodded. *Three out of ten.*

Liao pushed it a little further. "And if that's not enough, we might have to relinquish some of our territorial claims and—"

"No!" shouted Wan. "Not a single square inch of Chinese territory, and that includes Hong Kong, Macau, Taiwan, and the South China sea. We *will* go to war before we concede our country. If we give up our territory, next, they'll want us to reduce our military."

"Not our *country*, General, only those parts we claim to be ours, and with which neither our neighbors nor the international community agrees. And yes, I was about to say we might even have to agree to military reductions," said Liao.

"That's treason," interrupted Tao with a smirk on his face. "I agree with General Wan. I'd rather go to war than sell out my country for food." Tao was the Chairman of the Central Military Commission, in other words, the Commander in Chief and a warmonger.

"I'm not a military strategist, Huan, but I know Napoleon said an army marches on its stomach. Going to war with no food to feed the troops, not to mention having to fight the enemy while at the same time suppressing the domestic rebellion which Admiral Deng talked about earlier? No offense intended, Huan, but to me, that sounds monumentally stupid."

Tao was on his feet, red in the face, pointing his finger at the president. "I'll not be lectured by you. You should never have been president. In times like this, we need someone with a backbone. Not a damn jellyfish!"

Lang got to his feet. "Enough, comrades! This came as a big shock to all of us. We need time to process it. I propose we adjourn for one week. By then, we'll have more and better information. Let's use the time to carefully study what we have and think of solutions. A week from today, we'll come back here, and everyone will get a chance to present his solution."

Huan dropped back in his chair, still glowering at Liao with disdain.

One by one, they all started nodding in agreement. From their body language, Liao got the impression that Generals Lang, Jin, and Admiral Deng Jie, might still be in agreement with him. It didn't escape him that Generals Zeng Jiahao and Wu Shuren glanced at Dai Min to see what he was doing before they nodded as well. After all, he was in charge of 350 nuclear warheads.

Still three against seven. Maybe.

"Good," concluded Lang. "Now, can we agree that nothing of what was discussed here tonight will leave this room?"

Liao said, "The Standing Committee has to be informed. We can't—"

"Not until we have a plan," interjected Tao.

The Communist Party Congress (CPC) determined who would lead the people of China. The CPC delegates elected the Central Committee of about 200 members. The Central Committee, in turn, elected the 24-member Politburo, and they selected the seven-member Politburo Standing Committee, China's top decision-making body.

A few minutes later, Jin's speech-to-text program had transcribed the recording, and he handed each of the attendees back their flash drives with a text copy of every word that was said in the meeting and a copy of Minister Mao Xinya's report to the president.

General Lang phoned his wife and gave her the age-old, "Something urgent has come up at the office. I won't be coming home tonight." That was a lie. He was going to spend the night at Feng Lin's house. He had an extremely urgent message to get to his handler, the man whose name he didn't know, with the big black dog whose name he also didn't know.

In the back of his official car, on his way home to his adoring wife, General Jin Ping thought she would like it if he took her on a surprise visit to Hong Kong for the weekend.

In his private study at the residence in Zhongnanhai, President Liao was replaying the meeting in his mind. He couldn't help but think about the future of his country and his party. The Chinese Communist Party would not survive this, that much Liao was sure of. His dilemma was how to make the transition without obliterating the people of China in a war and famine.

His thoughts were interrupted by a text message from General Lang requesting a meeting first thing in the morning. He was intrigued and accepted.

Chapter Twenty-One

URGENT MESSAGES

Beijing, China

Lang left Feng Lin's house early on Friday morning after Lin had served him breakfast and ordered his driver to take him to Zhongnanhai.

After Lang had left, Lin watered the pot plants on the kitchen windowsill and swapped them around with the plants from the back porch, which started blooming a few days before.

One of the people passing her house that morning was a middle-aged man on a bicycle who passed this house on his way to work every weekday morning for the past ten years. He was one of a few who noticed the beautiful red flowers in the kitchen window brightening up the façade.

When he got to his office, he took out his cellphone and phoned his wife to let her know he was going to be about an hour late that night as one of the clothing stores near the office had a big sale on and he wanted to go and buy himself a new shirt for work.

Well, actually, that's what he told the woman who answered the phone. But she told him he must have the wrong number because her name was not Darling, and she had no husband. The man apologized profusely, the woman accepted his apology and disconnected.

The man checked the number, saw he had touched quite a few wrong digits, shook his head, and admonished himself loudly. He then concentrated on dialing the correct number.

General Lang didn't get much sleep. His mind was too busy processing the shocking news about the famine. He was in the president's office in Zhongnanhai at 7:00 a.m. Since becoming a spy for the CIA, with the help of the long-suffering Feng Lin, he had cut back on his excessive drinking, and his brain was functioning much better for it.

The transcript of last night's meeting was on its way to his handler. Last night was the first time in a very long time Lang Jianhong had stopped thinking about himself and started thinking about his country and her people. One thought that settled in his mind when he heard President Liao talking about the impending crisis was that the worst possible strategy would be to start a war. He was one of the generals who believed that China had more than just a good chance to beat America and the world into submission in a war—if everything played out as planned. But now, even thinking of starting a war while a famine of the extent Liao had described was raging was raving madness.

That was Lang's opening statement after he had taken his seat in the president's office.

Liao agreed and explained to Lang that China already

had to deal with slowing economic growth, an aging society, and a rapidly shrinking birthrate—the result of the one-child policy. "And now this—the total destruction of the economy and the starvation of our people. China will be thrown back to the 1970s when we were among the poorest countries in the world. One must be completely and certifiably insane to even contemplate going to war now. Yet, as you saw last night, that's exactly what the majority of your colleagues want to do.

"Just think about this for a moment. As the stockpiles run empty and the livestock is slaughtered, and the food disappears off people's tables, there will be a rising rebellion. The hungry masses will be desperate. Police, teargas, water cannons, rubber bullets, batons, not even real bullets or tanks will stop them when they're faced with starvation. The party members will abandon us in droves, our soldiers will desert and side with the proletariat. We would be the lucky ones— we would die with full bellies."

Lang's voice had dropped to a whisper. "Twenty million died during World War One, seventy million during World War Two. With modern weapons, excluding nuclear, the casualties will approach if not exceed one billion. And that would be before the famine would claim its share.

"The US has more than six thousand nuclear warheads, and we have three hundred and fifty. Worldwide there are more than thirteen thousand eight hundred warheads. Enough to blow our planet out of the solar system, if not the universe, several times over."

Liao had a wry little smile on his face. "I thought one could only die once."

"Is this the end of Chinese communism?" asked Lang.

"I don't know, but I can tell you in modern history, one-party regimes haven't lasted much longer than seventy years. The CCP has been in power since 1949, that's seventy-one years. There are only three countries where a single party ruled for longer than seventy years. The Soviet Union's Communist Party ruled for seventy-four years before the 1991 collapse. Mexico's Institutional Revolutionary Party ruled for seventy-one years until the 2000 elections. And North Korea, since its founding in 1948, is still headed by the Kim family dynasty. So, statistically speaking, we're getting to the end.

"Some scholars say the CCP is a smart authoritarian regime because we understand the threats to our power and mitigate those. We've always controlled the information we make available to the populace and suppressed free speech but managed to keep them happy by improving their quality of life through vibrant economic growth, building a moderately prosperous society, and reducing poverty.

"But history shows empires that overspent eventually find themselves on the day of judgment with debt. And debt is barbarous. Repay the debt, or it destroys you, no mercy. Governments could paper over their financial misdeeds for only so long before debt would demand its day of reckoning.

"Our declared government debt has surpassed the five trillion-dollar mark—more than forty-eight percent of the country's GDP. But that's a lie; the actual debt has already passed the thirteen trillion-dollar mark, two trillion more than the size of our entire economy."

Three hours later, when General Lang left the president's office, he had a totally new perspective about the challenges facing his country. One thing stood out above all else, to overcome those challenges, the reign of the seventeen marshals had to be ended. But right now, it would require a miracle.

Shortly after Lang had left Zhongnanhai, about two hours after receiving a call from a man who thought she was his wife called Darling, Feng Lin went shopping.

That evening after work, the man who had dialed the wrong number that morning and spoke to a woman who he thought was his wife went to a clothing store near his office to buy a new shirt for work. He paid in cash, and with the change, he received a complimentary 8GB SanDisk mini-SD card in its wrapper. The cashier told him, "We pick one customer randomly every day to receive a surprise gift. You're our lucky customer today."

The man thanked the cashier, went back to the office to pick up his stuff, and go home for the weekend. On the way out, he stopped by the office of the CIO (Chief Information Officer) to wish him a good weekend and hand him the mini-SD card.

Hong Kong

By the time the lucky man who won an 8GB SanDisk mini-SD card arrived home; General Jin and his wife had landed in Hong Kong on a commercial flight from Beijing. An hour later, they were in their room at the popular Peninsula Hong Kong hotel. After unpacking their bags, they took a shower and dressed up fancy for their dinner at the hotel's upscale French restaurant, Gaddi's.

At 8:00 p.m., the maître d' welcomed them at the entry to the restaurant and led them to their reserved table. Jin's instructions were to book into this hotel and go to this restaurant and bring the flash drive with the information with him. He assumed he would be approached by someone he would recognize.

Shortly after being served their drinks and entrées, Jin's attention was drawn to two couples following the maître d' to a reserved table next to theirs. The snail he'd just put in his mouth got stuck in his throat, and he started coughing violently.

He had met them one week ago at the Venetian on Macau Island, and ever since, he had hoped he would never have to see them again in his life. It was the Asian man Xu De, an agent of the Macau Commission Against Corruption, and the beautiful Italian woman, Marina, who he thought he was going to seduce, and the FBI agents Reynolds and Wiley. And that mean-looking big black dog. He was sure those were not their names. It didn't matter; he would've resented them just as much, no matter what their names were.

By the time the group had reached their assigned table, Jin had managed to wash the oily snail down with half of his white wine and assured his wife that he was okay. Despite all the noise he'd made, none of the group paid him any attention. They didn't even make eye contact when passing by his table. The dog, however, let out a soft growl in passing as if to say, "Just to let you know I remember you, and I'll be watching you."

Jin had lost his appetite. The snails fried in garlic butter, which had always been his favorite, seemed to be too rich for his system tonight. But it could've been the arrival of the four with that bad-tempered dog. He pushed the plate away and took a few more sips of white wine before excusing himself to go to the bathroom.

As he passed the table of the four with the dog, he put

his hand in his pocket and retrieved his handkerchief. The Super-Mini USB flash drive, about the size of his thumbnail, made no sound as it dropped on the carpet next to the dog.

An hour later, when Jin and his wife left the restaurant, the group who had spoiled his dinner was just starting on their dessert. The dog was asleep on the floor but opened one eye when Jin and his wife got up, sighed, and went back to sleep.

Chapter Twenty-Two

A DOOMSDAY SCENARIO

Matz Island, Hong Kong

The Daltons and Farleys were guests of the Matz family on Matz Island, and that's where they returned to after the dinner at Gaddi's. They were in a hurry to get back to the island to look at the information on the flash drive. It must've been important if Jin wanted to deliver it on such short notice.

When they arrived back on Matz Island, Jethro said he was about to call them to let them know he had received an encrypted file from his IT manager in the Beijing office, and it contained distressing information.

In Jethro's study, they soon discovered that the document on the flash drive from Lang was the text version of the audio recording on the flash drive delivered by Jin earlier. They listened to the audio file, and Tamara translated for the benefit of the Farleys.

Within twenty minutes, they got to the part where the attendees were peppering Liao with questions. Rex asked

Tamara to pause the recording so that he could call John Brandt.

John answered immediately. Rex didn't even bother with greetings or a report about the contact with Jin earlier. "John, get your IT guy to check the server. Catia is uploading three files right now. Two are text files. One is a transcript of a Trustees meeting that took place last night. The other is a report by Mao Xinya, the Minister of Agriculture and Rural Affairs. The third file is the audio recording of that meeting. I suggest you and whomever else are going to listen to it pour yourselves double, maybe triple shots, of the strongest alcoholic drinks you can lay your hands on before you start listening."

"That bad?"

"Much, much worse than bad, John."

Ten minutes into the recording, John et al. knew Rex had not exaggerated.

Oval Office, White House, D.C.

Two hours later, Howard Lawrence and Martin Richardson were with the president in the Oval Office. Within twenty minutes, they were joined by the rest of the members of the CWC (Cold War Council).

"My first thought is," said the president, "if just one idiot gets it in his head to turn this into a bioweapon well... If this fungus can contaminate China's soil and wipe out their grain crops, it could do the same to ours and the rest of the world."

The president didn't have to elaborate. This was a doomsday scenario. Meteorites, earthquakes, volcanoes, viruses, nuclear weapons, and such were the stuff thriller movies and novels were made of. Doomsday famines, not so much. Yet, a famine of these proportions could easily relegate any of those to a minor nuisance.

"My next thought. Leaving China to its own devices is not an option."

Everyone agreed.

Lawrence said, "Within twelve months, China will have no grain to feed their people or their animals. If the pathogen can be contained in China, the world could feed them. Globally we produce fifty percent more food than is needed. But if this thing gets out of China, our entire planet is doomed."

The DNI Tia Chapman said, "Mr. President, this has only one of two outcomes if it is contained in China; they either go to war to get food for their people, or they negotiate for it. If the crop failures become global, then it will be, as Howard said, we're doomed, the entire planet will be at war with each other."

Lauren Woods, the Secretary of State, added, "But our first challenge will be to get China to admit that they have a problem. And then to convince them to come to the negotiating table."

"Well, at some stage, they'll *have* to come to *a* negotiating table. Either to the one where they negotiate for food now or the one after a devastating war to negotiate for peace and food," said the president. "The US will have to take the lead on this. But Congress needs to understand that there'll be no time or place for brinkmanship, grandstanding, bipartisanship, or any other antics."

Tia said it for them all, "That, Mr. President, might prove to be more of a challenge than getting the Chinese to the negotiation table."

Everyone was smiling but knew many a truth is spoken in jest.

"Mr. President," Martin said, "it's important that we don't confront China with this information yet or tell anyone else about it. If we do, the Trustees will know they have a mole problem. They'll find them and execute them. And we'll have no idea what's going on inside the cabal after that—"

"You're not suggesting we do nothing, are you, Martin?"

"No, Mr. President, not at all. I'm only suggesting we keep this under wraps at least until after the Trustees' next meeting. We have to wait and see which way each of them is leaning. I suspect there will be two factions—hawks and doves. By the looks of it, Liao will lead the doves, Tao the hawks. In the meantime, we have six days to get the doves enough support to carry the vote if it comes to that."

"And how do you..." the president started but stopped because he knew to ask a spook such as Martin Richardson what his plans were would get him the same answer as asking the chair on which he was sitting. Except that the chair wouldn't lie. He was still trying to figure out how Richardson managed to recruit Deep Mantis and Dusty Wolf, the two Trustees, and stop the assassins in Taiwan.

"Martin is right. We have to wait, at least until after the next meeting of the Trustees. If there's nothing else, I suggest we pause the meeting and resume at eight o'clock tomorrow morning.

"Yeah, I know life's a bitch. Sometimes you have to work on Saturdays."

Everyone enjoyed the bit of mirth amid so much doom and gloom.

Chapter Twenty-Three

FIVE AND A HALF DAYS

Secured international video conference

On the call were Howard, Martin, John, Christelle, and Ollie from Langley, the Daltons and Farleys from Matz Island, and Yaron Aderet from Tel Aviv. And, of course, Digger and Cupcake. Even though they were not often, if ever, asked for their opinions, they seldom missed meetings, just in case their opinions *were* needed. These meetings would've been mind-numbing were it not for their kongs filled with treats.

Martin gave them an overview of the meeting with the CWC at the White House, which ended less than an hour before. "We expect two groups will emerge at the next Trustees meeting—doves and hawks. We're reasonably sure Liao wants peace. Deep Mantis and Dusty Wolf will do as we tell them, so, at the very least, Laio has two supporters. He needs five more, and we have to get them for him before the next meeting. Over to you, John."

John looked at the clocks on the wall. "Three o'clock

Saturday morning in Beijing. Five and a half days until the next Trustees meeting on Thursday at seven p.m. Let's start by listing all the ideas that come to mind and then discuss them."

"I need to have a quiet word with Lang as quickly as possible," said Rex. "He might be able to tell us exactly who we could target. And as leader of the Trustees, he might be able to buy us more time."

"We could use Stardust (Senator Jordyn Lancaster) to whisper a few very bad things about Tao Huan into the ears of her handler," suggested Ollie. "That might get a few of the marshals to rethink their support for him."

"Maybe someone should remind Generals Dai Min and Wan Huang about their collaboration with the CIA to get rid of Liao's predecessor," said Christelle.

"Another idea that comes to mind is the Politburo," said Ollie. "Liao is the chairman of that outfit, but he's hiding critical information from them at the moment. I'm wondering how pleased they'd be with their president if they find out about it?"

"I remember Lang told us that Liao was elected as president with the support of ten out of the seventeen marshals," said Catia. "I'm wondering how many of the remaining seven would be supporting Tao. He needs only nine marshals on his side to affect a palace revolution. We have to find out how many of the seven are on his side."

Everyone smiled when Josh said, "We could, of course, persuade a few of Tao's supporters to throw themselves off tall buildings after stabbing themselves in the back a few times."

There were no more ideas.

"Okay, let's decide who needs to do what, when, where, and how," said John.

An hour later, the meeting was over, and everyone had their assignments. The Daltons and Farleys would fly to Beijing, where Rex would set up a meeting with Lang. Yaron would ask Jethro to get in touch with Dai Min to warn him that his collaboration with the CIA a year ago had been leaked. Ollie was going to prepare Stardust for the meeting with her handler. Ollie's idea of letting the Politburo know that the Trustees were withholding vital information from them was worth pursuing and assigned to Christelle. Josh's idea of neutralizing some of the Trustees was parked for the moment—it could be used as a last resort.

Chapter Twenty-Four

NOT WHAT, WHO?

Half an hour after the video conference had ended, Rex got a call from Greg Wade, the head of CRC's IT team on the Ranch. Greg's team was a small but highly skilled group of IT specialists. Essentially, they were computer hackers, among the best in the business. With a few keystrokes, they could create havoc, blackout a city, take control of its traffic lights, enter government and corporate databases, access the bank records of any individual and organization, penetrate firewalls, break encryption, and much more. Since the establishment of Operation Peregrine, Greg's team had been working closely with their IT team. Sun Yan, codename Flat Arrow, had been embedded in Greg's team shortly after he had defected to America about four months ago.

After the greetings, Greg said, "I thought you might want to know that Lang has left Beijing on a plane departing from the military airport at Xijiao. He left about twenty minutes ago, and he's heading south at the moment. Could be Hong Kong."

Greg's GPS tracking software installed on the mobile phones of Generals Lang and Jin and Colonel Dong's had been sending their location coordinates to the CRC Cyber Room. Within a few days, Greg's team had plotted the locations of their targets' homes, offices, routes they traveled, and every other place they'd been to.

"You're right. I definitely want to know about that. Is Dong with him?"

"No, he's at home."

"What about Jin?"

"At home as well."

"Can you give me a quick rundown of Lang's movements since seven p.m. Thursday?"

"Yep. One sec, let me pull it up on the screen... Here you go. Between seven and nine Thursday night, he was at Zhongnanhai. Then he went to Feng Lin's house and spent the night, it seems. He left there at six yesterday morning and went back to Zhongnanhai and stayed there for three hours. A little after nine in the morning, he went to his office and spent the day there. At six yesterday afternoon, he went home. He left his home this morning at four-thirty and went to the Xijiao military airport."

"Thanks. Please email the log to me. And let me know as soon as you can determine where he's going."

"Will do."

In Langley, Lydia Andrews, the FBI liaison officer on the Peregrine team, had managed to get hold of Stardust before she headed to New York for the weekend. She and Ollie drove over to the Philip A. Hart Senate Office Building on Constitution Avenue in D.C. to meet with the senator in her office and brief her for her next meeting with her 'handler' the Chinese Cultural attaché, Song Yuhan, which was going to take place on Saturday night in New York.

On Matz Island, Rex, Catia, Josh, and Marissa studied the log of General Lang's movements emailed by Greg.

"Who did he meet with for three hours at Zhongnanhai so early on Friday morning?" Josh wondered.

Rex shrugged. "I think Liao and Tao are canvassing for support. So, my guess is that Lang has met with one or both of them."

Just then, Rex got another call from Greg. "Hey, boss, we thought your general was heading for Hong Kong, but his plane has landed at Qifengling, a military airport near the city of Guilin, Guangxi province. He got off the plane a minute or so ago."

"Thanks, keep the tabs on him, Greg. I want to know exactly where he's going."

"On it. I'll keep you posted."

Within minutes Catia and Marissa had their laptops out, Googling everything they could get about Guilin. The city, also spelled Kweilin, formerly Lingui, has 4.7 million inhabitants and is located in the northeast of China's Guangxi Zhuang Autonomous Region in the Lingui district. The Li River flows through the city. The topography of the area is marked by karst formations formed from the dissolution of soluble rocks such as limestone, dolomite, and gypsum. Deep erosion of the limestone plateau has left a multitude of tall needle-shaped pinnacles from which trees sprout improbably. These magnificent mountains have long been memorialized in Chinese paintings and poetry. In the seventh century, it was one of the major centers of Buddhism, and to this day, it boasts many famous monasteries. It is, without doubt, one of the most picturesque places on earth. A popular Chinese saying, directly translated as 'Guilin's scenery is best among all under heaven,' suggests as much.

"All very interesting," murmured Catia, "but what's there that could be of interest to Lang?"

"I'm pretty sure he's not taking a holiday," said Josh.

"Maybe he's going to meditate in one of the Buddhist monasteries in the mountains for the weekend," said Marissa.

Thirty-five minutes after Lang had deplaned, Greg was on the phone with Rex again. "Okay, he has been airlifted from the airport by a helicopter, I presume. His GPS coordinates show he's at a secluded spot along the Yulong River. Hang on, Rehka is checking out the location on the satellite images."

Rehka was the daughter of Rex's friend from Bilaspur, India. Rex and Rehka had met when he and Digger liberated her and six other women from a Saudi Arabian international black-market arms dealer and human trafficker. She had a master's degree in computer sciences and exceptional skills in programming and online research. Since she had met Greg Wade and worked with him and his team on several missions, her knowledge and abilities had gone from strength to strength, and so had their feelings for each other.

"Got it," said Rehka. "It's an old, abandoned Buddhist monastery. The area for miles in every direction seems to be deserted. No roads or buildings. No signs of humans."

Marissa smiled, "I told you he wants to meditate."

Rex shook his head, "He's not the meditating kind..."

"What's there, general?" whispered Catia, deep in thought.

A Cheshire cat-like grin broke across Rex's face. "Not what, who?"

"Huh?" Interjected Josh.

"Maybe another mistress?" said Marissa.

"A Buddhist monk?" Catia ventured.

"Something like that," said Rex. "If I'm not mistaken, we found the abode of Zhì Zhě, the Wise Man."

"No shit, Sherlock," said Josh incredulously. "And how did you figure that out?"

"Speculation, my friend. Pure speculation. Zhì Zhě is the Trustees' advisor. I think Lang is there to get advice."

Everyone was staring at Rex. Greg and Rehka had gone quiet.

Marissa was the first to look at Digger, followed by Josh and then Catia to see if he would be able to tell them if Rex was fooling around. But it was clear if Digger knew, he wasn't going to tell. He had a look on his face that resembled one of his smiles which could have meant anything, including, "You heard what Rex said, pay attention; I think he might be onto something."

"Guilin is about three hundred miles from here. With one of Jethro's planes, we can be there in an hour," said Josh.

"Don't get on the plane yet," said Rex. "I want to talk to John first. Maybe he can arrange for a keyhole-class satellite to be assigned for surveillance."

Chapter Twenty-Five

HE MIGHT BE CAMERA-SHY

Marissa dialed John's secured satellite phone. It was 10:00 p.m. in Langley; he and Christelle were still awake.

Rex told John about Lang's trip to Guilin and the theory that the purpose of the trip was to meet with Zhì Zhě. And suggested that a keyhole satellite be assigned to have a look at the location as quickly as possible.

John didn't need any convincing. He agreed to call Martin, who'd need the director's signature, and it could be done within an hour.

"Now, tell me something that I've meant to ask you for a while," said John. "You've been showing more interest in this wise guy than anyone else. What's it that you know or suspect that the rest of us don't?"

"I can't put my finger on it, John. The man obviously plays a big role in the plans of the Trustees. Maybe what got me curious in the beginning is that we have the names of everyone involved in the MK Plan, except for the most important contributor, who goes by a pseudonym. And then there's the fact that Lang lied when I asked him about Zhì

Zhĕ. I have a feeling he might play a pivotal role in the decisions the Trustees are going to make in the next few days. It would be good to know who he is."

"Agreed," said John. "I'll get hold of Martin and let you know when the satellite has been assigned."

Christelle chimed in, "You must have thought about a name, Rex?"

"Yes, ad nauseam," said Rex, "but I still have no idea." It was not entirely true; for the past hour or so, Rex had a gut feeling about the man's identity, but it was crazy. There would be no harm done if he waited until he had confirmation.

"Okay, we might know soon," said John. "I suggest you cancel your planned trip to Beijing and make arrangements for a quick trip to Guilin if the satellite can't give us what we want."

Less than an hour after John had made his request to Martin, the keyhole satellite had been instructed to focus its cameras on the coordinates of Lang's mobile phone and started streaming images to the Peregrine analysts in Langley and Catia's laptop. John, Christelle, Cupcake, Ollie, and Martin were in the Peregrine ops room connected via video link with Rex and the team in Jethro's study on Matz Island.

It's only in movies where one can make a satellite camera zoom in until the freckles on the nose and color of the target's eyes can be seen. On satellite images with a one-meter resolution, each pixel on the image covers one square meter on the ground. Google Maps has a fifty-centimeter resolution. The best commercial satellites have a twenty-five-centimeter resolution. Spy satellites generally have a five-centimeter resolution making it possible to see people but not make out their faces. The CIA keyhole-class satellite, which looked down at Lang's location, had a one-centimeter resolution, not enough to see eye color or freckles but enough to recognize faces.

About three hours after Lang's mobile phone had arrived at the secluded monastery, a man in a dark suit carrying what looked like a briefcase emerged from the front door. He took a few steps, stopped, and turned back to the figure standing in the front door as if talking to the person, but the cameras couldn't make out any of the features of the person in the door.

"Now, on the count of three, I want you to look up," whispered Catia to the man in the suit standing outside the monastery more than three hundred miles away. "One... two... three... now."

He ignored her command and kept on facing the person in the door.

Rex was about to say something witty to Catia when the man looked up at the cloudless sky toward the south. And then the approaching military helicopter came into view.

"Bingo!" she shouted.

Rex laughed. "A bit of lag in the signals, it seems. Now, do you think you can use that same magic to make the person hiding in the shadows of the front door come out?"

Catia laughed as she waved her hands slowly in front of the screen, chanting some magic Italian rhyme from her childhood. But the mystery person remained inside.

"Antisocial jerk," Josh scoffed. "Obviously, his mother taught him no manners, or he forgot them. It's polite to accompany your guests outside when they're leaving."

"I think he might be camera-shy," said Rex.

"Well, then we have to pay him a visit," said Josh.

"Agreed. What do you say, John?"

"Yep. Start packing. Martin, can you make sure the satellite stays focused there?"

"Will do."

The facial recognition software at Langley had been given the twelve faces of the Trustees to compare with the images from the satellite first. It took the computer less than a minute to decide with eighty-two percent certainty that face belonged to General Lang Jianhong. No surprise there.

Chapter Twenty-Six

BIRD WATCHING IN THE LINGUI DISTRICT

Four hours later, the Daltons and Farleys arrived at Guilin International Airport onboard one of Jethro's business helicopters. Rex and Catia traveled on their French EU passports as Rowan and Catherine Donnelly. The Farleys traveled on American passports as Jason and Miranda Carlson. Their passports were stamped with ten-year multiple-entry visas—useful for repeated travel between Hong Kong, Macau, and mainland China.

The customs official found no problems with their visas or Digger's papers. He displayed mild interest when they told him they were birdwatchers, welcomed them to China, wished them a pleasant stay, and expressed the hope that they would see many birds.

Any scrutiny of their luggage would have confirmed their claims of being bird enthusiasts and nature lovers. Camping equipment, powerful binoculars, top-of-the-range cameras, various lenses, and other birdwatchers' paraphernalia which included a few bird magazines and books. The four mini surveillance helicopters were disassembled, and the component parts, distributed among the four backpacks along with the camera parts and accessories. Other than multi-utility Swiss army knives, they had no weapons. But no one was interested in searching the luggage of a group of stinking rich foreign tree huggers with a dog on a bird-watching excursion.

They returned to the helicopter, and the pilot got clearance from the control tower for takeoff. It was 5:40 p.m., about one hour to sunset: enough time for a quick bit of sightseeing. They had been staring at the satellite photos of the monastery and surroundings on their laptop screens for hours; what they wanted to see now was what it looked like in reality.

About five minutes before sunset, the pilot dropped them off at a deserted campsite five miles north of the monastery.

As soon as the chopper had disappeared, Rex rigged Digger up with his full harness equipped with a video camera the size of a pencil eraser located on the top of his head, between his ears, and practically invisible. Everything Digger would see would also be visible to Rex. Mini earphones were fitted in Digger's ears, completely hidden, and a mini microphone, not much bigger than a pinhead, was fitted on the harness between his front legs. All of it was wirelessly connected to an iPad mini, which Rex held in his hand now but could strap to his forearm later.

He pushed his nose against Digger's wet nose and ruffled his ears. "Who's a clever boy?"

Digger yelped softly and licked Rex in the face wagging his tail in excitement.

"Okay, buddy, scout and hide." Rex made a slow circle with his finger in the air, and Digger disappeared into the jungle.

Although Rex never learned to give Digger proper commands, like military dog handlers do, over the years, working as a team on many missions, they had worked out a communications system between them which left some of Rex's colleagues with the notion that the two of them spoke some kind of 'language' which only they understood. In reality, however, it was Rex who had learned to be very attentive to Digger's body language at all times.

Everyone huddled around Rex, watching Digger's progress through the woods on the iPad mini screen.

Fifteen minutes later, Digger was back. The coast was clear.

Rex gave Digger some food and water while they had dinner consisting of energy bars and filtered water. Afterward, they shouldered their backpacks and headed out with Digger scouting a few hundred yards ahead of them. They moved slowly and silently. The terrain they had to traverse was tropical and rough. By Rex's and Josh's calculations, it was at least a three-hour hike. But they were in no hurry. They had until sunrise the next morning to get into position.

Chapter Twenty-Seven

WHAT WAS NEGOTIABLE AND WHAT NOT

Oval Office, White House, D.C.

Rex and his team had covered less than a mile by the time the subdued members of the CWC arrived for breakfast with the president at the White House on Saturday morning. No one had to tell them that wars are violent and harmful affairs and would create orders of magnitude more harm than only bombs and bullets when coupled with a lack of food.

The history of warfare is filled with military tactics used to starve enemy armies and civilian populations. During World War II, Nazi Germany had a 'Hunger Plan' aimed at starving twenty million people in the territory controlled by the Soviet Union. Fortunately, the plan never came to fruition, but hundreds of thousands did starve to death during the German siege of Leningrad (St. Petersburg) between 1941 and 1944.

One only had to look at the modern-day conflicts in

South Sudan, Syria, and Yemen to understand the devastating effects of food shortages during war.

According to the international relief agency Mercy Corps, nine million people die of hunger every year, more than twenty-four thousand per day, more than the death toll of AIDS, malaria, and tuberculosis combined.

On May 24, 2018, in an attempt to address the issue for the first time in its history, the United Nations Security Council unanimously passed a resolution condemning the use of food insecurity and starvation as a tactic of war. A noble gesture but with no clout to enforce it.

Notwithstanding the UN's resolution, the world was facing a cataclysmic war caused by a catastrophic famine. The CWC members knew that to prevent that war from starting would require careful planning and shrewd diplomacy.

The first and most urgent step was to put measures in place to prevent the fungus from spreading beyond the borders of China. But that was much easier said than done. The PRC was not going to take kindly to international blockades to isolate and quarantine their entire country. If at all possible, it was best to leave that option as a final measure if all else failed.

Howard suggested that soil samples be collected in secret and smuggled to the US for scientists to study the fungus and develop a treatment. His suggestion was accepted.

Next on the agenda was how to get the PRC leadership to the negotiating table. The transcript of the Trustees' meeting three days ago didn't fill them with confidence that it was going to be an easy task. If they had to deal with the president and the Politburo, they had to establish diplomatic channels to work through. But the Trustees were a secret organization with terrifying powers in the PRC's political hierarchy and military. And that was only the ten marshals among the Trustees. There were seven more marshals, known to be saber-rattlers, who were not part of the cabal but who could easily join forces with some of the ten to oust President Liao. They only needed the votes of nine marshals to kick Liao out.

The last thing the world needed now was a belligerent Chinese president, such as Tao Huan. For a peaceful solution to the crisis, the majority of the seventeen marshals had to be persuaded, by any means necessary, short of assassinating Tao, to support Liao.

The final item on the agenda was to consider what was negotiable and what not. Obviously, the US and the rest of the world were in a position of strength, but only if the fungus stayed in China. Nevertheless, one of the first things to be agreed upon was to allow the world's scientists to work with their Chinese colleagues to find a treatment. And that China would agree to keep their borders closed until the pest has been eliminated.

Undoubtedly, the USA and its allies were going to be the major contributors to the food provided to China. Therefore, it would be the ideal opportunity to talk about the South China Sea, human rights abuses such as the oppression of the Uyghurs, Christians, and other religious groups, border and territorial disputes with Tibet, India, and others. The status of Taiwan, Hong Kong, and Macau should also be on the table. And so should China's production of fentanyl, stealing of intellectual property, and manipulation of their currency. And last but not least, the reduction of their military and nuclear arsenal.

Chapter Twenty-Eight

WATCHING THE MONASTERY

Sunday morning, Guilin, China

Rex et al. arrived at the monastery two hours before sunrise. The stars and half-moon in the cloudless sky provided enough light for their night vision equipment to give them a good view of the monastery from their hideout about two hundred yards away. Rex reported their arrival to John in Langley.

The place was dark. Digger made two trips around the property but found nothing of interest.

Catia took one of the two mini-drones from her backpack and assembled it. Marissa had two more in her backpack. They were mini-helicopters and measured a little over six and a half inches in length and a little more than one inch in width. They weighed less than thirty-three grams without batteries. The three onboard cameras: one looking forward, one looking straight down, and one pointing downward at forty-five degrees, had night vision and thermal imaging capabilities. They were also equipped with

159

long-wave infrared and day video sensors that transmitted video streams or high-resolution still images to their base station within a range of two and a half miles. The drones could reach speeds of up to twenty-nine miles per hour and stay in the air for half an hour on a single charge.

She launched one of them and steered it to the building, keeping it about two hundred feet above the ground. It took her less than ten minutes to declare that the thermal imaging camera on the drone showed that there were only two people inside the monastery, both asleep in the same bed.

From the satellite images, they already knew that there were no fences or guards around the property. Digger's reconnaissance trips and Catia's drone confirmed that and the fact that there were no dogs either. From the footage supplied by Digger's camera and Catia's drone, it was evident that the place was small compared to other monasteries. It was ancient but had been altered recently to make it inhabitable for the current occupants.

An hour before sunrise, the Daltons left the Farleys behind in the hideout on the north side of the building and made their way around to a hideout on the southwest side overlooking the courtyard.

And then the waiting started. They were hoping that Zhě Zhì might be an early riser who liked to take an early morning stroll around. But they knew the man could just as well like mid-morning or mid-day or late-afternoon walks. Or he might be so camera-shy he wouldn't set foot outside his monastery in the daytime. On the other hand, maybe he didn't even like walking. They had given themselves thirty-six hours from the time they'd left Hong Kong, and they'd already used sixteen hours just to get into place.

The four of them were in communication with each

other through their Molar Mics. They didn't have a contin-
uous connection with the Peregrine team in Langley, but it
would merely be a matter of pushing a button on any of
their satellite phones to establish a connection.

By 7:00 a.m. Sunday morning, almost an hour after
sunrise, none of the occupants of the monastery had come
outside.

Marissa launched a drone and navigated it to hover over
the building at about four hundred feet and reported that
the thermal images showed one of the people inside seemed
to be sitting at a table in a room at the back of the building.
"Probably Zhě Zhì in his study," she said.

The other person, probably his wife, was busy in what
seemed to be the kitchen. On closer inspection of the courtyard, Marissa detected something among the plants that
caught her attention. She zoomed the camera in and soon
realized she was looking at no less than four cleverly camou-
flaged satellite dishes pointing skyward. "For TV and inter-
net, I presume."

Chapter Twenty-Nine

STARDUST'S DINNER DATE

Saturday evening, New York, USA

It was 7:00 p.m. Saturday in New York when Senator Lancaster arrived at the Le Bernardin, the elite French restaurant on 155 W 51st Street, New York, for her dinner date with Song Yuhan, who was convinced he was her handler, and she was spying for the MSS.

In the Peregrine ops room in Langley, Martin, John, Christelle, Ollie, and Lydia Andrews were listening and watching. They knew Song was recording the meeting, and they were happy that he was doing so. They wanted the exact conversation to reach the MSS in Beijing.

Three tables away from the senator and her companion, was a couple staring into each other's eyes as if the secret of eternal happiness could be found there. They were FBI special agents in plain clothes. Outside, in an unmarked car, were two more special agents listening to the conversation at the senator's table.

"You asked me to get the information about Yuan Lee's

interrogation," Lancaster said after their main dishes were served. "I managed to get it, but let me tell you, I took a big risk. I hope this was the last time you're going to expect me to do something as dangerous as this."

"You know I can't promise you that."

"I reserve the right to refuse your damn requests when I think it's too dangerous—"

"Senator, maybe I should remind you of our conversation last time; you no longer have the privilege of doing that. You'll do as you're told, or you'll be taking your meals inside a maximum-security prison for the rest of your life."

"You should stop threatening me like that. You're making me depressed. One of these days, I might start thinking of throwing myself into the path of a bus."

"Senator, you're worth much more to us alive than dead and outside of prison rather than inside. And we'll do everything to keep you alive and out of prison, but you'll do well to remember that sometimes the juice is not worth the squeeze. So, as long as you make it worth our while, we'll look after you and protect you."

Lancaster almost smiled at the thought of how much fun she was going to have the day when she was going to watch the FBI arrest this son of a bitch. "Okay, I'm sorry, but it's not easy for me to do this. It's stressful."

Song took a sip of his wine. "Apology accepted. I understand it's not easy for you. But it's because you are missing the big picture. What you are doing is important for the future of both our countries and the world. Your current president is steering our nations toward war. You can prevent it. That's how you should see it."

"Great. That's how I will see it then. Beats feeling like a traitor all the time."

Song ignored her sarcasm and said, "Now, tell me what you've found out about Yuan's defection."

Ollie understood the principle that a good lie consisted of mostly truth and very little untruth. That's why he and Lydia Andrews had briefed Senator Lancaster with the actual facts except for adding one name and leaving a few bits out.

The senator had no idea what was true or false in her brief. She was given to understand that all of it was true. That way, Ollie could be sure her body language couldn't betray any of the lies in the narrative.

"Yuan Lee says it was Tao Huan, the Chairman of the Central Military Commission, the head of your military that forced him to defect."

"Really?" Song was stunned.

"Well, according to Yuan, Tao has presidential ambitions. He hated Li Lingxin with a passion and was looking for an opportunity to get rid of him. Then, somehow, Yuan doesn't know how, the CIA became aware that Li had been working on a secret plan to release a lethal virus, developed by Yuan's bioweapons division. Somehow, again Yuan doesn't know how, they, the CIA, got word to Tao about it. He saw it as the opportunity he had been waiting for. But he needed irrefutable evidence.

"So, he confronted Yuan about his homosexuality. Although it turned out to be a bit more than just homosexuality, Yuan actually prefers underaged boys. And Tao knew all about it, even had photos and videos of it. To make a long story short, he blackmailed Yuan into handing him President Li's plan and all the information about the virus. In exchange, Tao worked with the CIA to get Yuan out of China and defect to America.

"Yuan speculates that Tao then went to the seven

marshals who opposed Li and told them what Li was up to. The seven marshals convinced some of the marshals who supported Li to switch sides. The new coalition of marshals then got rid of Li Lingxin."

Song nodded. "Who's your source?"

Lancaster stared at him for a few beats and then, with a slight grin on her face, slowly raised her middle finger.

Song didn't even attempt to pursue the matter. He changed the subject. "Who on our side is working for your side?"

Now that was the question every one of the Cold War veterans on the Peregrine team was hoping and praying Song would ask.

Anyone who graduated from spy school knew that was one of the most dangerous questions to ask an informant. If the informant was truthful, no problem. The effect would be that the spies in your midst will be exposed and dealt with, and the enemy would lose their advantage.

But if the informant was not truthful, the results could be devastating. A case in point is James Jesus Angleton. He was the chief of CIA Counterintelligence from 1954 to 1975. The KGB fed him false information about a KGB mole working inside the CIA. Angleton spent the rest of his working life on an intensive mole hunt inside the CIA; it was a fruitless and destructive hunt for someone who never existed. All that Angleton achieved was to paralyze and almost destroy the agency. To the day the KGB was disbanded, they regarded Angleton as their best agent ever.

Stardust had been briefed to expect the question. "Well, I told you about Tao Huan. The codenames Aurora and Falcon were mentioned in passing during the discussion about Yuan Lee. I was too scared to ask for real names. Though, I picked up that they are marshals in the PLA, one in the air force and the other in the rocket force. They apparently assisted Tao in getting Li out of office. Oh, by the way, there's a lot of speculation that Li didn't die of a heart attack but of a bullet to the head. Do you know if that's true or not?"

Song obviously had no knowledge of that; he was unsettled and tried his best to hide it. He shook his head and took a sip of wine.

In Langley, John and company were high-fiving. As soon as this information reached the Minister of State Security, he would have no choice but to report it to President Liao.

On the Ranch in Arizona, a former employee of Unit 61398, Flat Arrow, who had intimate knowledge of the MSS's computer networks, started monitoring the MSS servers for the arrival of the information package from Song Yuhan in New York.

Chapter Thirty

AND ZHĚ ZHÌ IS...

Sunday afternoon, Guilin, China

It was not a picnic to watch a monastery while hiding in a jungle in sweltering heat and soaking humidity. All kinds of insects, flying and crawling, and spiders couldn't believe their luck when they discovered the all-you-can-eat smorgasbord right on their doorstep.

A few minutes past midday, Digger's soft growl came through in Rex's Molar Mic. Digger was hiding among the bushes and trees on the west side, about thirty yards away from the low wall of the courtyard.

"What's up, buddy?"

He replied with another soft growl.

"Show me, buddy. I can't see a thing."

There was some blurred movement on the iPad mini's screen strapped to Rex's forearm as Digger crawled into place so that he and Rex could see what it was he had heard and smelled a few seconds ago.

About forty seconds later, the images stabilized, and Rex

said, "Stay. Watch and hide." He could see the inside of the courtyard now. A man was sitting at a table under a big tree. But the camera on Digger's harness was not powerful enough to make out the man's facial features in the dark shadows. A minute or so later, an oldish woman came out with a tray loaded with what looked like food and drinks, placed it on the table where the man was sitting, and took the seat opposite him. Her face was not familiar.

"Catia, Marissa, the Wise Guy, and the missus are in the courtyard. Each of you get a drone over there as quickly as possible," said Rex.

Within minutes Catia and Marissa each had a drone overhead filming from all possible angles. They got a lot of footage quickly but not good quality because of the deep dark shade below the tree and the risk that the noise of the drones would be heard if they brought them down too low.

After about thirty minutes of frustration for the camera crew, the mystery man left the table and walked to the side of the courtyard, where he stood and stared out over the valley below.

Through his binoculars, Rex recognized him almost immediately. That was the face he had expected to see. Even so, he was still surprised when he got the confirmation. "Do anyone of you recognize him?" Rex asked.

One by one, they reported in the negative.

"Have another good look. I'm sure I know who he is, but I don't want to influence your judgment."

Marissa and Catia had to concentrate on piloting their drones and couldn't pay attention to much else. But Josh could zoom the lens of his monocular in on the face. "Shit! How the hell... Rex, is that who I think it is?"

Rex chuckled softly. "Buddy, I learned a long time ago not to try and figure out what is going through that twisted mind of yours. But if you're thinking that guy is supposed to be dead and his ashes scattered over the South China Sea, then there is hope for you."

Catia said, "Marissa, I think our boys have lost their marbles."

"Okay, ladies," said Rex, "have a few more minutes of fun with your toys, then we'll pack up and meet at the extraction point."

An hour later, at the extraction point in a valley two miles west of the monastery, Catia had a drone up to keep a watch, and Digger was out scouting on the ground. Marissa had her laptop out and started uploading the footage captured by the drones to Langley.

Rex got his satellite phone out and powered it up to call John. A few seconds after the phone was linked up to the satellite, a text message appeared on the screen. It was from Jethro.

"Looks like we're off to Beijing next. Jethro says Lang has requested an urgent meeting."

"Great," said Marissa. "I'm sure there will be fewer creepy-crawlies hell-bent on dragging me off to their nest while I'm still alive." Now she had time to study the face of the mystery man closely. A few minutes later, she said, "Catia, I've got good news; our boys have not lost their marbles. That guy *is* who they say he is."

Slowly Catia looked up from her laptop screen at Marissa. "*Dio mio...*," she whispered. "Can you imagine the international repercussions?"

Just then, John answered Rex's call. It was 1:45 a.m. in Langley.

"What's up, Dalton?"

"Our Wise Man's real name is Li Lingxin."

The silence that followed was so long Rex checked the screen of his phone to make sure he was still connected.

Then John started laughing.

"What's so funny, John?"

"Sorry, Rex, I'm still a bit sleepy. For a moment, I thought you said the guy's name is Li Lingxin."

Rex frowned. "That's exactly what I said, John."

Another long silence erupted on John's end. "This guy has the same name as the dead former Chinese president?"

"No, John, this guy *is* the former president, and he's undead."

"U-n-d-e-a-d... you mean... like... "

"*Mon Dieu.*" That was Christelle.

There was a sharp bark. That was Cupcake.

"Are you *sure* about this?" That was John.

"Look at the videos and run the facial recognition to convince yourself, but we're sure that's him."

Everyone could hear John take a deep breath. "I'll be damned."

"I suggest you wake up a few people and have a look at the videos. We're at the extraction point, but I haven't summoned the pilot yet. Oh, and Jethro left a message; Lang wants an urgent meeting."

"Ok, sit tight. I'll call you back soonest."

When the call ended, Catia said, "Rex, I got the impression you knew all along who we were going to find in that house?"

"Only since yesterday when we decided that Lang was probably visiting Zhě Zhì, I started remembering a few things. One thing led to another..."

"Of course they did. As they always do when Rex Dalton is involved," mumbled Josh.

"Well, I remembered the whole world saw the man's state funeral, but no body was displayed or entombed as they did with all previous PRC presidents.

"Then I remembered how Lang lied when I asked him who Zhì Zhě is. Why would he lie? What's so important about this guy that he would sell out his country and coconspirators to save his own ass but protect the identity of this man?

"The penny finally dropped as I remembered when I asked Lang how Li died. He told me Li shot himself. But while he was talking, I saw he was hiding something. At the time, I thought maybe one of the marshals shot Li, and Lang was hiding that from me. But it was only yesterday that I realized this is what he was hiding."

Forty-five minutes after John had disconnected the call with Rex, John, Christelle, Cupcake, Ollie, Martin, and Howard were in the Peregrine secured meeting room connected through a secured and encrypted satellite link to Rex's satellite phone.

"You were right, Rex. The facial recognition software has no doubt at all. The man in the video footage captured by the drones and the former President of China is one and the same person," said John. "The computer is still trying to figure out who the woman is. We know it's not his wife. She's living in the lap of luxury in a very nice house in the best neighborhood of Beijing."

"It's like being handed an information superweapon," said Ollie.

"Precisely. The question is when and how to use it," said Martin.

"Right," said Howard. "And that's why we need to go and see the president immediately."

Minutes later, Howard and Martin were on the way to the White House to wake up the president. It was 2:30 a.m. Sunday in D.C. and 2:30 p.m. in Guilin.

Chapter Thirty-One

NOT MY PREFERRED OPTION

Sunday morning, Oval Office, White House, D.C.

The President was used to being aroused at all hours of the night to make decisions about crises around the globe. When the secret service agent knocked on the bedroom door and woke him at 4:15 a.m., the first thought that went through his mind was China. Beijing had been one of the major causes of distress during his presidency, but for the past few days, they had become his number one stressor.

While listening to Howard and Martin, he was going through the emotional states of unbelieving, skepticism, and then excitement as expected. After all, he *was* human. Those were the emotions experienced by all other humans who had received this news the past few hours.

"Okay, I'd like to hear your ideas about how we can use this to our advantage. All ideas, good, bad, ugly, even the crazy ones."

Howard said, "Mr. President, obviously it would be extremely embarrassing to the PRC government if the rest of the world heard about this. But more effective than threatening to embarrass them in front of the international community could be to use the information to destroy the Trustees by showing the Politburo what's been going on right under their noses."

"I like both ideas, especially the second one if we can pull it off," said the president, "but that might mean the end of Liao. And if he is dethroned, Tao might take over. Not a desirable outcome at all."

"Mr. President," said Martin, "the thing is that we don't know where Li stands on this famine issue. We believe that was on the agenda at yesterday's meeting between him and Lang. We hope to get the answer to that within the next twenty-four hours. If Li is going to side with Tao Huan, we might be forced to consider radical measures."

"Such as?"

Martin had to fight back the temptation to tell the president about Josh's suggestion. "Sir, we could take him out of the picture."

The president wanted what all presidents wanted: a second term and a proud legacy. Abducting or assassinating another country's president, even a supposedly dead former president, was a sure way to make him a one-term president with a disgraceful legacy. Notwithstanding, the president didn't reject Martin's idea outright. "It's an option. Not my preferred option, but if that's what it will take to prevent a war, then I'll make that call and live with the consequences."

Twenty minutes later, the chopper was on its way to pick Rex and his team up and take them back to the airport from where they would be flown to Beijing on Jethro's Gulfstream G550.

Chapter Thirty-Two

THE NEGOTIATIONS HAVE ALREADY STARTED

Sunday evening, Beijing, China

Rex and Digger arrived at Feng Lin's house at 10:00 p.m. He was in his Asian disguise as before. Catia, Josh, and Marissa, and three of Jethro's guards, kept a watch on the house and neighborhood. Rex was in communication with them through a Molar Mic, and Digger was rigged up as before with mini microphones hidden in his collar. In Langley, also tuned in was the usual crowd consisting of Martin, John, Christelle, Ollie, and Cupcake. The latter hard at work to get the peanut butter that was stuffed into her kong.

Although Rex had urgent questions, he decided to let Lang talk first. Lin wasn't required to be at this meeting; she served the men tea and pastries and retired to her bedroom.

"Before we continue," said Lang, "would you mind telling me what your name is?"

Rex smiled. "My friends call me Badger." He could already hear Josh giving him a mouthful about that name.

Lang grinned knowingly; he was not going to push Rex

for an honest answer; he had far more important matters to address. "Okay, *Mr. Badger*, as you can imagine, the news that our president brought to the meeting on Thursday night was earthshattering."

"I can imagine it must've been," Rex said. As far as he knew, Lang didn't know about Jin Ping's recruitment or that Jin had provided an audio recording of the meeting. Lang had no need to know, not yet.

"What I saw Thursday night has shocked me. Tao and his cronies are insane. They're not thinking about our country or her people. Tao wants to be president, and he doesn't care what it takes. He has support among the seven marshals who didn't vote for Liao in the beginning, but we don't know how many of them. He only needs nine marshals to throw Liao out. Right now, we are sure he has the numbers."

"We?"

"I had a long meeting with President Liao on Friday, and it has opened my eyes to the catastrophe facing our country under President Tao. Liao has convinced me that we must stop him. But for that, Liao needs to get the support of the majority of the marshals. You might find it strange, but I've become convinced that it's time to end the marshals' hold on our country."

Rex was skeptical. Lang was a ruthless and shrewd man. Not to be trusted. He had been watching the general carefully for any telltales of deception, and he had been watching Digger, who had been sitting right in front of the man staring at him. But he saw nothing to alert him. Lang was either the best deceiver Rex had ever seen, or he was honest. He decided to give him the benefit of the doubt, for now. In the spy business, it often happens that people become disillusioned with their government and decide to work against them in the hope of building something better.

"Does the president know that we have the Middle Kingdom plan?"

"Yes, I told him all about it."

"Including that you've been working with the CIA and that we know all about your coming food crisis?"

"Yes."

"How do you plan to stop Tao and break the marshal's chokehold?"

"I don't believe in God and the divine foreordaining of all that will happen. However, I'm at a loss to explain it as anything other than predestination that America got the Operation Middle Kingdom plan in their hands when they did. You are our only hope of survival."

If the military doesn't want you anymore, you could make a killing as a salesman. Rex almost smiled at that thought. "What do you have in mind?"

"There are two parts to it. Firstly we need your help to keep President Liao in his seat. Secondly, we need your help to feed our people. If Liao gets kicked out and Tao gets in, we'll still need your help to feed our people, those who survive the war."

"Right."

"And it goes without saying we understand that you'll have certain conditions. We're ready to talk about them when you are."

Rex was nodding slowly. Contemplatively. "From what I've seen in that transcript of your Thursday night meeting, Liao doesn't have the support to stay in power."

In Langley, Howard was on the edge of his seat. He was looking at Martin. "Tell him not to make any promises. We need to get some firm undertakings from them first."

John shook his head. "No, we're not going to get in his ear unless it becomes absolutely necessary. Dalton knows what he's doing."

It was as if Rex heard that conversation. "General, I think before we discuss anything else, we need to talk about your president's plans for the future. You see, in America and other parts of the world, people were excited when he became president. We thought he was a man of peace, a proponent of a free market economy. But eight months later, to our utter dismay, we discovered he was plotting with ten marshals to take control of the world. And you're the chairman of that evil caucus.

"Now that you're staring at the chasm of famine, you're expecting America to come to your rescue. You've been undermining us for decades. You've been stealing our manufacturing jobs and our intellectual property. You've been sending us your spies and fentanyl. You've been hacking our computers and our online identities. General, you've worked out a plan to annihilate America. You were busy executing that plan when you were interrupted by an inconvenient famine. You've chosen us as your enemy. You've started the war. I can carry on, but why should we even consider helping you?"

Howard blew out a long-held breath and smiled. "Attaboy. Give him hell, Rex."

Lang took a sip of his whiskey while staring at Rex. "Of course, you've got every right to be circumspect. But let me give you a bit of background information. The hundred-year plan was adopted by the CCP in 1949, and every Communist Party Congress since then has reiterated their commitment to it. Every president is expected to support the plan and take steps to ensure it comes to fruition by no later than 2049, preferably earlier.

"However, what very few people outside the innermost circles know is that the hundred-year plan has lost its allure for some of the highest-ranking officials in this country. And their numbers are increasing. Liao has been one of them for a long time, and I am a recent convert."

"Yet both of you are members of the Trustees who started a war with America to destroy us so that you could control the world? I say, Chinese man speaks with forked tongue."

Lang was shaking his head. "We want to negotiate an end to the war."

"You mean you want to surrender?"

"Precisely."

Rex smiled. "Now that sounds like a good idea to me. It's a pity I am not authorized to accept the PRC's surrender. But tell me, General, be honest, would we be having this conversation now if China had enough food?"

"Probably not now, but in the not-too-distant future, yes —after the war."

In Langley, John looked at Howard and said, "Surrender is so much better than firm undertakings, don't you agree?"

Howard smiled. "Touché."

Digger had dropped from his sitting position onto his belly and sighed. Probably because he was happy that Lang was not trying to deceive his alpha. But it was also possible that he was tired of sitting and staring at the man that posed no threat or deceit.

Rex took notice. "Okay, let's leave that there for the moment. Which of the marshals supports Liao at this moment?"

"We're almost sure of Admiral Deng Jie, the commander of the PLA Navy."

"So, Liao has you and Deng, maybe?"

"As you can see, we need all the help we can get."

"It seems to me you need a miracle and not a small one either. Moses's parting of the Red Sea comes to mind."

Lang had a blank look on his face.

Rex didn't have time for a Bible lesson. "The four most senior marshals are you, Wan, Dai, and Deng. We already know Wan and Dai are on Tao's side."

"Yes. And Dai Min holds sway over Generals Zeng Jiahao and Wu Shuren. They will go whichever way he goes."

"Okay, let's say a miracle happens, and you get six of the ten marshals among the Trustees; what about the seven who are not Trustees? They didn't support Liao in the first place. So, if only two of the remaining four Trustees vote with the seven non-Trustees, Liao is out."

"I know it looks like a lost cause. But we can't give up."

Rex had been briefed by John and Ollie about the dinner Stardust had with her handler and the false information she'd given him. If that information lands on Liao's desk, as John et al. intended, he could use it to get Generals Wan and Dai on his side. But Rex was not going to let Lang know about that yet.

"You'll have to give me an idea of what you think it is that we can do."

"Well, you recruited me to work for the CIA. Do you have more like me?"

"I wouldn't know, but I'll pass your request on to my superiors. Even so, I can assure you no one will lift a finger until there's an agreement in place, and I'm afraid they might not be inclined to negotiate such an agreement with you."

"Why not?"

"For starters, you're not an elected official. You're not even a member of the Politburo. As far as we're concerned, you and the rest of the marshals are rogue generals of the PLA who have been meddling in your country's political system since the CCP came to power in 1949. In our opinion, you're a de facto junta."

"In other words, you want the president to put his hand on paper?"

"I guess that might be a good start. But it might be worth keeping in mind that it's also entirely possible that my government might not even *want* to negotiate with Liao. After all, he's been part of a secret, illegitimate coterie bent on destroying America. They might prefer to deal *directly* with the Politburo."

Lang sighed. "It sounds as if the negotiations have already started. I'll pass the message on to the president."

"Good. I've got only one more matter to discuss."

"What?"

Chapter Thirty-Three

HE HAS ENORMOUS INFLUENCE

Sunday evening, Beijing, China

"What did Zhĕ Zhì have to say about all of this?"

Lang's eyes shot wide for a fleeting moment. He drew a deep breath.

Digger sat up and stared at him.

Rex said, "General, let me warn you. Don't lie to me again. I know who he is, but I'm giving you the opportunity to come clean now and show us you're serious about finding a solution for your country's problems."

Lang avoided Rex's gaze as he stared at the floor for a long while. Then whispered, "Who told you?"

"Nobody. I've got proof right here." Rex tapped on his satellite phone. "Start with his name and tell me the whole story."

"He's our former president, Li Lingxin. And you might find it hard to believe, but Liao is totally unaware of his true identity. The one time Liao met him, Li was disguised as a very old man. But Tao knows who he is."

That was a big surprise to Rex, but he remained poker-faced. The revelation did, however, set Rex's mind racing with ideas of how that information could be used in the future.

"That night, when your president confronted Li with the evidence of the virus he was about to unleash, we were ten marshals, the ten who became known as the Trustees, who went to his office and confronted him with the evidence provided by Yuan Lee. When we arrived at Zhong-nanhai, we didn't know that Yuan was already in America. Li told us about that.

"Li had no idea how Yuan got to America. But it was clear that he must've had some help. Our MSS only figured that out months later when they discovered that the CIA was behind it. One of the MSS's senior agents was tasked to find who in the CIA was responsible and who on our side helped them to pull it off. But that mission failed when the agent and his men were killed in a shootout with your FBI. So, we still don't know who betrayed us."

Rex managed to keep an impassive demeanor. That agent and his men killed a CIA disguising expert, Yasmin Burke, and almost killed Josh and Marissa. Were it not for Digger, who led him and Catia to the house where Josh and Marissa were being tortured, they would've been dead.

"Be that as it may," Lang continued, "Li showed us his version of the hundred-year plan. It was clear that his plan could've worked if only he waited until we had a vaccine or cure for the virus. The fact that it had already reached epidemic proportions in Shanghai, he thought, was good for us, despite the fact that the scientists told him a cure was years away, if ever. But Li thought it would keep the world off our backs if we also got hit by the virus. We couldn't let him do it."

"Not to mention the fact that Li's biggest transgression was that he didn't involve all the marshals in his plans?"

Lang made no reply.

"But you felt the rest of his plan was solid; you just had to adapt it. So you cooked up this scheme to make the world think Li has died. And then you put him up at that monastery outside Guilin from where he orchestrated the development of the Operation Middle Kingdom plan, right?"

"How do you know where he is?"

"I was there yesterday."

"You've been watching me?"

"Of course I have. But that's beside the point. Where does Li stand on this?"

Lang was shaking his head. "It's sad, but I think he is delusional. He's in love with his own plan. China will conquer the world. He thinks the famine will not happen, that the world will fall over their feet to feed us because they fear us. His hate for America and your president for humiliating him borders on insanity. Not even the fact that America knows all about his plan brought him to his senses. He even thinks this might be an opportunity for him to make a comeback from the grave. I wasted my time yesterday."

"And you've also put yourself in a precarious position."

"Why?"

"You told him we have the plan, and you told him you support Liao, didn't you?"

"Yes."

"He's going to tell Tao about it—"

"Damn! That was a big mistake."

"Right."

"I'll have to get Li out of the picture, quickly."

"I take it there's nothing that prevents Tao from meeting with Li?"

"He can't talk to Li unless either General Dai or I arrange the meeting and one or both of us is present."

Rex didn't think it was necessary to respond; Lang knew what had to be done.

In Langley, Martin smiled. "Good work, Rex. You've just saved POTUS from making the decision to remove Li from office, again."

In Langley, John flipped the switch on the microphone and told Rex, "Take a three-hour break. Lang needs to brief Liao, and we need to brief you."

Rex had only one more question. "Who is the woman with him? I know she's not his wife, well not the one he was married to at the time of his faked death."

"She's a courtesan, Ding Cui. We have arranged with her to live with him, and she knows who he is."

Shortly after midnight, Lang was on his way to the president's residence at Zhongnanhai, and Rex was heading for the hotel. He and his team had already gone two days without sleep, and the end was not in sight.

Chapter Thirty-Four

AND WE HAD NO IDEA

Monday morning, Beijing, China

Fifteen hours after Senator Lancaster's dinner date ended, Shen Delan, the Minister in charge of the MSS, received an alert about an urgent for-your-eyes-only message awaiting him.

Song Yuhan, who reported directly to Shen, was one of his most senior agents working out of the Cultural Office of the Chinese Consulate General in New York and the handler of one of the MSS's most prized assets, Senator Jordyn Lancaster.

A few months ago, a mission in the USA to get their hands on a top-secret intelligence database had failed miserably. In the aftermath, Shen had tendered his resignation to the president. But the president had refused to accept it, and Shen considered himself a lucky man to still be in his position.

But now, as he read the report and listened to the recording from Song, he was all but sure that he was not going to survive this ordeal. Part of the MSS's job was counterintelligence. One of his department's most important responsibilities was to rat out spies, and in this case, they'd failed spectacularly.

After the defection of Yuan Lee, it took the MSS a few weeks to put some pieces of the puzzle together and figure out how the Americans did it. A senior agent was put on the case to track down those responsible and kill them. That operation ended in failure when the agent and his men were killed. That mishap cost Shen's predecessor Xuan Bai his job, probably his life—he disappeared. The problem was that they still didn't know who helped the Americans to get Yuan Lee out of the country. That's why Song was tasked to get the information from Senator Lancaster.

As he listened to the recording of the meeting between Song and Lancaster over and over, he wished he had never instructed Song to get the information. He rewound the recording for probably the tenth time and pushed the play button.

"Well, I told you about Tao Huan. The codenames Aurora and Falcon were mentioned in passing during the discussion about Yuan Lee. I was too scared to ask for real names. Though, I picked up that they are marshals in the PLA, one of them in the air force and the other in the rocket force. They apparently assisted Tao in getting Li out of office. Oh, and by the way, there's a lot of speculation that Li didn't die of a heart attack but of a bullet to the head. Do you know if that's true or not?"

It didn't take Shen long to figure out that Aurora could be none other than General Dai Min, in charge of China's nuclear arsenal, and Falcon, General Wan Huang, commander of the Air Force. The information was devastating. Tao Huan, Chairman of the Central Military Commission, the head of the military, the second most powerful man in China, a traitor? Two of the most senior generals in the PLA traitors?

"And we had no idea," he mumbled.

It was after 1:00 a.m. when he phoned the duty officer at Zhongnanhai to make an appointment with the president. He was given a fifteen-minute slot at eight in the morning.

Shen had no idea that 6,500 miles away on the Ranch in Arizona, Flat Arrow took note of the appointment and told his manager, Greg Wade.

We have to do it

Monday morning, Beijing, China

In their hotel room, while Rex and Josh scanned the room for bugs and deployed countersurveillance equipment, Marissa used her secured satellite phone to establish a secured video connection to the Peregrine ops room in Langley. Catia brewed strong black coffee.

John's smiling face came into view on Marissa's laptop screen. "Dalton, every old spook around here agrees that you put on a masterful performance tonight. Well done."

Rex was a bit embarrassed, and it got worse when Josh, Marisa, and Catia started clapping their hands and shouting, "Hear! Hear!"

"And I would like to make special mention of his choice of moniker," said Josh. "Badger, a small but tough animal that can knock an entire colony of bees senseless with its farts and steal their honey. Brilliant choice, Rex."

Rex raised a middle finger slowly in front of Josh's face as everyone roared with laughter.

Digger let out a soft yelp, which Catia interpreted as "And what about my performance?" She laughed and filled his kong with beef jerky. "Thanks, Digger. Rex couldn't have done it without you." That made Digger very happy—the praise and the kong.

Martin said, "Howard and I kept POTUS up to date throughout the meeting. He said he would be willing to have a secret personal meeting with Liao. We advised him to wait and see what Lang brings back from his meeting with Liao. So, we're leaving it with you to decide when the best time is to let Lang know about it."

"Okay."

Martin nodded for John to continue.

"We have confirmation that Shen Delan, the minister in charge of the MSS, received the recording of the meeting that Song had with Stardust and that he has scheduled a meeting with Liao for eight o'clock this morning.

"Greg has already sent you the recording of the meeting between Song and Stardust. The part you want to listen to starts about half an hour into the recording."

"Okay, thanks."

"Shen will tell Liao that Tao, Dai, and Wan are traitors. Liao can use that information to get Dai and Wan on his side. I leave it to you to make us smell like roses for being so helpful."

Rex smiled. "That shouldn't be too difficult. We're saints."

"But things don't look very rosy for Liao, though," said Martin. "By my count, Liao could get the votes of Dai, Wan, Deng, and Jin, as well as Zeng Jiahao and Wu Shuren, that's if Dai can influence them. With Lang that makes seven, giving him the majority among the Trustees, but that leaves ten who could vote for Tao."

"And don't forget five of the seven votes will be obtained through extortion," said Ollie. "Not exactly what I would call a loyal following. Nevertheless, if that's what's required to keep Liao in power, we better start looking for more corrupt or peace-loving marshals."

"Well, for the corrupt kind, he doesn't have to look far," said Josh. "Didn't the ten Trustees conspire together to mislead their country and the world about the death of Li Lingxin?"

"Now there's a usable idea," said Ollie.

There was no recording to play for President Liao but, his heavy drinking notwithstanding, Lang still had a reasonably good memory. Besides, it was not so difficult to remember the most important outcome of the meeting—the Americans wanted to negotiate the terms of surrender before they would help.

Lang spent about fifteen minutes giving his president a fairly comprehensive overview of the meeting with the man who called himself Badger and his big black dog.

"So, they want me to put pen on paper and tell them I want peace and what I'm prepared to pay for it?"

"Yes, it's our terms of surrender, so to speak, Mr. President. If they like what we offer, they'll help. If not, they might go to the Politburo. I suggest the quickest way to get this done is a personal meeting with their president."

"Let's put that in the letter, and instead of listing what we are prepared to negotiate, let's tell them what's not negotiable. That list will be much shorter than the other one."

Lang was still trying to figure out how to solve the Li Lingxin dilemma, but he couldn't discuss it with the president.

Two hours later, Lang left Zhongnanhai with a letter addressed to the President of the United States, signed by the President of the People's Republic of China. It was written in English; after all, President Liao had a Ph.D. from the University of Cambridge.

Lang was still trying to figure out how to solve the *Digger* dilemma, but he couldn't discuss it with the president.

Two hours later, Lang left Chongnanhai with a hand-delivered, the President of the United States, with the People's Republic of China, ... without including the president Liao and the Chinese ... ... reference ...

Chapter Thirty-Five

A LETTER SIGNED BY THE PRESIDENT

Monday morning, Beijing, China

The meeting between Rex, Digger, and Lang resumed shortly after 3:00 a.m. Rex had the same security and communications in place as before.

Lang handed Rex the letter addressed to the President of the United States. Rex took his satellite phone out, took a picture of the letter, emailed it to Howard, and dialed his secured phone. Howard was in the Situation Room with the president and the rest of the CWC members. Howard answered right away. "I have in my hand a letter addressed to the president. I've also emailed it to you. Should I read it to you?"

"Yes, go ahead."

It was not a long letter. It was handwritten in black ink on the official presidential stationary. Liao's handwriting was elegant and easy to read.

Beforehand Rex had speculated that the contents would probably be a long list of what would be negotiable and what not. But this letter was written by a man in great despair, in essence, an unconditional surrender.

Dear Mr. President,

No doubt you have been fully informed about the circumstances that gave rise to this letter.

In light of the gravity of the threat of a catastrophic famine that might spread beyond the borders of China exacerbated by the real prospect of a global holocaust caused by a war which some of my countrymen want and the time constraints we are operating under, I am of the opinion that it is essential for us to meet at your earliest convenience.

Given the terrible consequences either event holds for the Chinese people and the American people, and the rest of the world, I intend to come to the meeting with only China's sovereignty as non-negotiable.

I am ready to meet when you are, Mr. President.

In the interim, until we can meet and establish direct channels of communication, I have authorized General Lang Jianhong to act as my liaison.

Sincerely yours,

Liao Qigang

President of the People's Republic of China

The President of the United States and the CWC members had the same take on the contents of the letter as Rex. This was a cry for help from a desperate man.

The president told Rex to let Lang know that the invitation to meet had been accepted. President Liao would be informed as soon as the necessary arrangements had been made.

The call ended, and Rex passed the president's message on to Lang.

It was impossible to miss the relief that washed over Lang's face.

Only in an advisory capacity

Monday morning, Beijing, China

"Now, let's talk about how you're going to get President Liao the votes he needs to stay in power."

Lang took a long deep breath and let it out slowly in relief. "Does that mean you're authorized to help?"

"Yes, but only in an advisory capacity." Rex was lying; he had orders to do whatever it takes, including extreme measures, to get nine marshals on Liao's side. But his orders were also to let Lang and company handle as much of it as they were capable of.

"You have my full attention," said Lang.

Rex told him that Shen Delan, the Minister of the MSS, would be at President Liao's office at 8:00 a.m. to inform Liao that Dai and Wan were traitors.

"What! How the hell do you know that?"

"Not important, General, just take my word for it; that's precisely what Shen is going to say."

"But how... I mean, you must have infiltrated—"

"You're wasting time, General. Let's focus on how you can use the information to your advantage."

"My first thought is to arrest them."

"If that's what you want to do but—"

"You don't agree? What would you do?"

"I'd use the information to get their votes. If you lock

them up, you've only succeeded in taking two out of the equation. But if you win them over, voluntarily or otherwise, you have their votes and those of Dai's lackeys. That's four extra votes. That gives you the majority among the Trustees if you get Jin on your side."

Lang nodded. "I agree. That's the better way to do it."

Rex then told him exactly how Dai and Wan helped Yuan Lee escape. He gave him a lot more details than was in Stardust's report. Of course, Lang had no need to know about Rex and his team's involvement or about the roles Jethro Matz and David Sarlin played in the affair. He told Lang that Shen would also report that Tao was the mastermind behind Yuan's defection. But Rex explained it was a piece of planted misinformation.

"Why did you drag Tao into it?"

"It seemed like a good idea. But perhaps it could be the last resort if you can't get enough votes for Liao before the next meeting? You could, for instance, order the MSS to arrest Tao shortly before the meeting."

Lang smiled and nodded.

"For now, I suggest you do nothing about Tao; let him think he has all the votes he needs. And the marshals who support Liao could make Tao believe he has the support of everyone."

Lang was still smiling. Things were looking a lot rosier than a few hours ago. "I see your people thought of everything."

We have to. We're trying our best to save the world, you dimwit. "General Jin Ping," said Rex, "Liao is seeing him sometime this morning, right?"

"Yes, at eleven-thirty."

"Well, I've heard a bit of gossip, which might be helpful. A friend of mine has a friend who is good friends with one of the owners or managers at the Venetian Macao Resort Hotel and casino. Apparently, the MSS, FBI, and Macau corruption unit ran a joint sting operation for counterfeit money launderers a week or so ago and caught Jin Ping in the act. I don't know all the details, but I thought maybe Liao could ask Jin to tell him the full story."

Lang was shaking his head. Not in disagreement but in bewilderment about how much the CIA seemed to know. "I will let the president know about that. So, now we need two, preferably three, of the remaining ten marshals. I'm hoping that once we have the first six onboard, they might be able to help us bring the rest over."

"That sounds good. I wonder if the fact that all ten marshals involved in Li's faked death, including you, are guilty of conspiracy and fraud and suchlike, could be helpful while canvassing for more votes?"

Lang stared at Rex in surprise. "I never thought of that."

Chapter Thirty-Six

THE NEW PRESIDENT OF CHINA

Monday morning, Beijing, China

As the Chairman of the Central Military Commission, Tao Huan was the Commander-in-Chief of the PRC's Armed Forces, the largest and second most powerful military force on earth. That made Tao a formidable man. He graduated from the PLA Academy of Military Science and came from a long lineage of illustrious military leaders. None of his ancestors had ever been the President of China, though—that would be his legacy.

Tao had a good military mind. But unfortunately, not the self-awareness to realize he neither had the insight into matters of state nor the statesmanship required to lead a country. He had a hammer in his hand; therefore, every problem looked like a nail to him.

He still felt humiliated that the marshals didn't select him as president when Li Lingxin was kicked out and instead went with the weak-kneed submissive Liao Qigang. Ever since, he had been working tirelessly to drum up support among the seventeen marshals for the day when an opportunity such as this presented itself.

Since the last Trustees meeting, he had been counting heads, and he was certain he had all the support he needed to call the seventeen marshals together to discuss the ousting of President Liao Qigang.

He had spent all of Friday and the weekend chasing down and meeting with the seven marshals who were not Trustees. In the process, he broke the undertaking he gave to not divulge any of the information discussed at the Trustees meeting seven times. He didn't care; he got seven votes.

Generals Lang Jianhong, Dai Min, Wan Huang, and Admiral Deng Jie were the predominant marshals in the ranks of the Trustees. Their juniors would follow their lead. Dai and Wan already showed their allegiances in the Thursday meeting. Although Lang and Deng were not so vocal as the other two, he could see no reason why he wouldn't get their support. But even if they didn't support him, he was only two votes short of a majority. Once he had the necessary support, he'd visit Li Lingxin to get his blessing, and in a few days, China would have a new president.

The three traitors

Monday, Beijing, China

Thanks to the information provided by Rex; General Lang was able to brief President Liao comprehensively before meeting with Minister Shen Delan of the MSS.

Liao was not a good actor, but with his natural inexpressive disposition, it was not necessary to act much to convey his shock and anger at hearing the news about the three traitors from the Minister.

"How reliable is this information?"

"Mr. President, we can't be a hundred percent sure until we receive independent verification. However, I can assure you that Song is one of our most senior and experienced agents. The informant is a Senior Senator, and she has been utterly compromised. Song has assured me she would not put a foot wrong for fear of what would happen to her if she lied to us. Even so, I intend to assign my best agent to verify the information. Nonetheless, at this stage, we have enough to be suspicious about, to put them under close surveillance, and to be careful around them."

Liao nodded.

"Mr. President, I can, of course, take them in for questioning if that's what you want?"

Liao had been thinking about precisely that for the past three hours since Lang told him about it. And he was tempted to give the order. It would've brought a swift end to Tao's career and an end to his challenge for the presidency. But Liao knew that was speculation on his part, wishful thinking even. In reality, the marshals would still have the power, they would appoint a new Chairman of the Central Military Commission in a day or two, and unless he, Liao, had the support of the majority, they might decide to clean house and appoint a new president while they're at it.

Liao shook his head. "No. For now, I don't want you to do anything other than to place them under close but surreptitious surveillance. Emphasis on the word surreptitious. Report their every move to me, and I mean every move; I want to know who they meet, when, where, and what is being said."

"Yes, Mr. President."

"Minister, do I need to tell you that not a single word of what we've discussed here will leave this office?"

"No, Mr. President, not at all."

"Good. Anything else?"

"No, sir."

"Thank you for bringing this to my attention so quickly. Stay on it."

"I will, sir."

Shen felt like kissing the president when he left the office. He couldn't believe that he was still a free man, not to mention still having his job. This man deserved his respect and loyalty.

Chapter Thirty-Seven

NOT TOO DIFFICULT A CHOICE FOR ME

Monday morning, Beijing, China

When Shen had left, Liao asked his chief of staff to summon Generals Dai and Wan to Zhongnanhai for an urgent meeting.

The generals were at a conference when the president's request came through. They told the caller they'd see the president in two hours after the conference was over.

Liao knew it was nothing but an act of defiance. It made him smile. Their wings were about to be clipped—very short—if not amputated.

The president was not entirely surprised when the wayward generals turned up fifteen minutes later than scheduled at 10:30 a.m.

They didn't apologize, and he made no mention of it either.

Liao offered them seats and something to drink. They took the seats but declined the drinks. He looked them in the eyes and said, "I received a report earlier this morning, which I've decided not to believe until I've had the opportunity to talk to both of you."

"What?" growled Wan and Dai in chorus.

Those were the last civilized words uttered by the two generals for the next few minutes as Liao laid out the accusations against them. They denied any knowledge, used colorful language, and made serious threats, including calling the marshals together to discuss who the next president would be.

Liao kept calm. During his time in the UK, at the University of Cambridge, he had seen Shakespeare's Hamlet a few times and couldn't help but remember those immortal words: *The lady doth protest too much, methinks.*

"Generals, I've instructed Shen Delan to investigate. He has strict orders to treat it as top secret. I suggest we let him conduct the investigation so that you can be cleared of all charges."

"Call him off," demanded Wan.

"I concur," said Dai.

"But I don't," said Liao.

"Don't what?" snapped Wan.

"Concur."

They were infuriated. After all, Liao served as president by their invitation, and this was insubordination. Fingers were waved again, profanities and threats were repeated. But Liao remained unnervingly calm and collected.

"Qigang, Yuan Lee is a homosexual, a child molester, and a traitor. Are you suggesting you're going to *believe* the scumbag?" growled Wan.

"I wasn't aware of Yuan's sexual predilections until I heard him telling the Americans all about it. As for being a traitor, he was quite explicit that the two of you forced him into it and that you cooperated with the CIA to get him out of the country." Liao was using a bit of liberty with the truth. He didn't actually hear Yuan say that.

"Lies!" shouted Dai. "All of it. Lies!"

"What the hell do you expect from a man who betrayed his country? Of course, he would tell them anything to make him look good," said Wan.

"I'm wondering how his admissions about his sexual weirdness would make him look good?" retorted Liao.

Dai did a double-take and swallowed hard when it dawned on him that Liao knew a lot more than he had alluded to so far. Liao was holding an ace up his sleeve, maybe more than one.

He and Wan were in over their heads—that much he understood. It didn't matter who the source of Liao's information was; everything he had said so far was accurate. Dai blinked a few times as it finally sunk in that this was all about getting their backing against Tao for the next Trustees meeting.

Dai also understood that Liao had two options: have them arrested or make a deal. Obviously, Liao preferred a deal; otherwise, they would have been in the custody of the MSS already. Their options, however, were limited to a choice between Liao and Tao or bullets in the back of the head. There was no telling how Tao would react to this news, but everyone knew he was a heartless and self-serving man. Liao was almost the opposite. Simple choice.

But Wan was still steaming with rage and not thinking clearly. "Believe whatever you want, Qigang, but take my word for it; you're going to pay dearly for this. Oftentimes since you've become president, I've regretted my decision to vote for you, but never more so than right now. This was the final straw. I'll see to it that you're relieved of your duties." He made to stand up.

"I'm sorry to hear that, General. The thing is, I know exactly what you did and how you did it. I don't think you've got any idea of how much trouble you're in. I was going to offer you a way out of the hole you've dug for yourself. But if you've made up your mind, then so be it."

Dai leaned over and tapped Wan on the arm. "Huang, sit down and shut up. You're not thinking properly. It's over. Clearly, Qigang knows the truth, all of it, and you and I are about to be arrested for treason."

Wan's anger was replaced by terror almost instantaneously. The blood had drained from his face when he turned back to Liao and sunk back in his chair slowly.

Dai continued, "Let's hear your offer."

Wan nodded in silence.

Liao suppressed a smile. "Our country is on the brink of the biggest disaster in its history. If we don't do the right thing and do it quickly, about half of our citizens, seven hundred million, *will* starve to death. And some of you marshals think it's the ideal opportunity to go to war, which would kill the rest.

"Here's what I want from you. You support my suggestion of negotiations and oppose the war. You use your influence to persuade the other marshals to follow your lead on this."

"In exchange for?" said Dai.

"One, not getting arrested. Two, closing the case with the MSS and wiping the records. Three, when this is over, you'll both go on early retirement. You'll receive your full pension, a generous bonus, and a heroes' retirement party."

Wan and Dai had what-do-you-think looks on their faces when they turned to each other.

Wan shrugged first. "Not too difficult a choice for me."

"For me either," said Dai as he turned back to Liao.

"Call off the dogs, and let's discuss how you want to go about this."

Liao managed to hide the relief that was washing over him.

The end justified the means

Monday morning, Beijing, China

At 11:30 a.m., when Generals Dai and Wan walked out of the president's office, General Jin Ping passed them on his way in. Jin had no idea what awaited him. Wan and Dai knew, but they had no idea what sins Jin had committed.

Liao was emboldened by his encounter with the two generals who had just left and cut to the chase the moment Jin was seated. "General, I've got only one matter to discuss, and that's your run-in with the authorities in Macau a week or two ago about money laundering. Tell me everything, and don't even think of lying. I know all about it."

Jin had gone ashen-faced. Did the president know he was working with the man with the big black dog? But he'd promised Jin that he was safe as long as he cooperated with them. He thought the man was CIA, but now he wasn't so sure anymore. It didn't really matter anymore, the president knew about it, and Jin was heading for an MSS interrogation cell.

Jin's usual showboating was absent as he explained to the president what happened. He admitted to the money laundering but made no mention that he had been trapped by the CIA and coerced into working for them.

"In other words, you've committed a serious crime?"

Jin swallowed. "Yes, Mr. President. It was—"

"A very stupid thing to do. I know. And by the sounds of it, not a one-off. You've been doing this for a while, right?"

"Yes, Mr. President. I'm—"

"Why shouldn't I call the MSS to take you into custody? Money laundering is a serious offense. It costs this country billions every year. It's economic terrorism, General."

Jin was shaking his head slowly as he whispered, "Please, Mr. President, It would—"

Liao raised his hand and stopped him. "Spare me the it-would-never-happen-again. I know it won't. I'm going to make sure of that."

Jin looked sick.

"But there might be a way for you to stay out of jail—"

"I'll do—"

"Anything I tell you to do. I know. So, listen carefully."

Liao told him what was expected of him from that moment until Thursday's meeting and beyond.

"I accept, Mr. President. You have my support."

"That's what I hoped to hear from you. And when this is over, you're retiring."

Jin thanked the president and assured him that he would not disappoint him.

At 12:30 p.m. Admiral Deng entered the president's office. His meeting stood in stark contrast to the meetings of the three generals who preceded him. The admiral had no shameful secrets. His support for President Liao was genuine. And so was his undertaking to have a quiet word with Vice-Admiral Shao Yong, the commander of the PLA submarine fleet, who reported to him.

By 1:00 p.m., Liao had the explicit support of five marshals, three more in the pipeline, and a mild attack of morality because he had to coerce so many of them into seeing things his way. Even General Lang, his most ardent supporter, had nasty skeletons in the closet. The only squeaky-clean supporter was Admiral Deng.

Nevertheless, Liao's streak of morality only lasted until he convinced himself that the end justified the means. It was a pity there were no more marshals with skeletons in their closets. Not that he knew of.

Politics is a dirty and unscrupulous business. That much Liao had learned in his time in office as a minister and as president. What he couldn't comprehend was that the marshals, the Deep State of China, the real power behind the throne, could be so brainless about the unimaginable suffering facing the nation.

Chapter Thirty-Eight

ON THE CAMPAIGN TRAIL

Monday afternoon, Beijing, China

Tao was on the campaign trail when he met Generals Dai and Wan for lunch. He was acutely aware that Liao was doing the same but unaware of the vastly different and much more efficient tactics employed by his opponent.

The generals knew there was no such thing as a free lunch and fully expected the question when Tao posed it about halfway through the main course.

"What's your solution for the problem Liao dumped on us last week?"

Dai said, "Let me put it this way, Chairman, only over my dead body will my country be traded away for a few bags of grain."

Wan nodded in agreement.

Tao had no training in lie detection. He was oblivious to the fact that he was being hoodwinked—big time. If he didn't make the mistake of underestimating his president, he would've put tabs on the Trustees. If he did, he would've known that the two generals had met with his rival only a few hours before, and he would have been a lot less gullible than he was now.

"So, you will be supporting me at the next meeting?"

"Absolutely," said Wan and Dai almost in chorus.

"Good. I knew I could count on you. Now, if the majority of Trustees vote against Liao, it's a vote of no confidence. He'll have to step down as president. What are your thoughts on that?"

"I don't see any problem with that," said Wan. "We make you president. You should've been president all along, not that jellyfish as you called him."

Tao was grinning from ear to ear. "I appreciate your support. With the support of the seven non-Trustees, which I already have, plus yours, we have enough to send Liao packing. I would, however, like to get broader support than just a one-vote majority. Things are too volatile if the margin is so small. The ideal would be to have the unanimous support of all the marshals so that we don't have another palace revolution a few months from now when we're in the middle of a war and famine and need strong leadership."

"I like that idea," said Dai. "We will go to work on the rest of the Trustees to get them on board."

"Thanks. Do you know where Lang and Deng stand?"

"We haven't discussed it with them yet," said Wan. "But why would they want to support a yellow belly?"

"I don't expect them to, but I'll have a word with them, just to make sure."

"Who do you want as your Chairman of the Central Military Commission?" Asked Dai.

"I think in the current circumstances, we must combine the two positions."

"Excellent. I was going to suggest that," said Dai.

"Good. That's settled then. One more thing I need to do is to inform Li about what's going on and get his support for this."

"Agreed," said Dai. "When do you want to see him?"

"Tomorrow morning."

"No problem, I'll make the arrangements."

Dai had no idea what a predicament he had just created for Lang.

Tao was an elated and confident man when the lunch ended. President Tao had a much better ring to it than Chairman Tao.

At 3:30 p.m. Admiral Deng arrived at Tao's office for his meeting. Again, Tao was uninformed about the fact that Deng had a meeting with Liao while he had lunch with generals Dai and Wan.

The meeting was short. Deng told Tao that he was deeply worried about the famine, but China could not afford to be weak now. "We have to stand firm, or the Americans and their allies will ruin us. We will lose our claims to the South China Sea. We will lose Macau, Hong Kong, and Taiwan. You have my support."

It was 6:00 p.m. when Tao finally got hold of Lang and asked him to come over to his office for a drink. He knew nothing about Lang's visit to Li on Saturday. However, he knew about the three-hour meeting Lang had with the president on Friday morning. He was dying to know what was discussed but refrained from asking directly.

"General, I take it you're as concerned about the famine as I am?"

"No doubts about that, Chairman. It's the biggest crisis this country has ever faced."

"What are your thoughts on how we should address the crisis?"

"Well, for starters, we can't afford to appear weak to the world. Of course, we'll have to negotiate for the food we need for our people, but we have to negotiate from a position of strength, not weakness. The world is scared of our military power. They'll do anything to avoid a war with us. That's our position of strength. Yes, we might have to lay off our plans for the South China Sea, Hong Kong, and Taiwan for a while. Definitely not sacrifice them at the negotiating table.

"I tried to get that through Liao's thick skull on Friday but to no avail."

Tao could barely suppress his smile.

"How much support does Liao have for his ideas?"

"As far as I can tell, he won't get a single vote for it on Thursday night."

"Good. I plan to call all the marshals together after Thursday night's meeting to talk about getting rid of Liao. I have the support of the seven external marshals, plus Dai, Wan, and Deng so far. Can I count on your support as well?"

"Absolutely."

"Thanks. I was counting on that. I'm off to see Li tomorrow morning to brief him about the situation. General Dai made the arrangements. I would like you to accompany us."

Lang wasn't expecting that. His stomach roiled. This would not only destroy their plan but also be the end of him. Yet, he managed to keep calm.

"No problem, I'll reschedule my appointments. What time?"

"Four tomorrow morning, from Xijiao airport."

"Good. I'll see you and General Dai at four then."

Lang all but sprinted to his official car. His plan was to move Li on Tuesday night. He'd spent most of the day working out the logistics. But now, Chairman Tao had thrown a monkey wrench in the works. He had to get Li out of there overnight, but there was not enough time to do it. Or... he could... assassinate him.

In the back of his car, he sent a text message to Feng Lin telling her he was on his way and ended with three smiley faces. That was the code for her to let the Badger know an urgent meeting was required.

Within minutes Lin had sent out a group text message with an attachment to her friends containing her secret recipe for the most popular Chinese dessert, sweet *nian gao*. Most of them replied immediately, thanking her. One of the replies came from a recently acquired friend, Wu Nuan.

Chapter Thirty-Nine

HIS PLAN WAS SIMPLE, DARING, AND BRILLIANT

Monday evening, Beijing, China

Shortly after 8:00 p.m., Rex and Digger were back in Lin's living room where a troubled General Lang was already waiting.

Lang told him that Dai and Wan had lunch with Tao and played along nicely as instructed by Liao. But then Tao said he wanted to see Li Lingxin the next day. Dai had not been briefed about the problem with Li and agreed to make the arrangements.

"I got invited to Tao's office for a drink. I did the same as Dai and Wan; I misled him about my support. That was all good and well until Tao told me he wants me to go with him and Dai to see Li tomorrow morning. Of course, I could say no, but that wouldn't change anything. With or without my presence, Tao is going to hear about my visit on Saturday and everything I told Li, including that I support Liao and the fact that America has the MK Plan in their hands."

Lang explained that his plan was to wait for Dai to be converted by Liao into a supporter, then go to the monastery the next morning with Dai, explain to Li that his life was in danger and that he and his courtesan had to be moved to safety. But now, there was not enough time to do all of that and be back in time to be at the airport to accompany Tao at four in the morning. Lang's head was hanging when he finished.

Rex was a successful operator because of his ability to rapidly assess a situation, form a plan, and execute it. Although Li's assassination would solve the immediate problem, he knew it was essential to keep him alive if they wanted to break the marshals' power over the country. And it was clear Lang was incapable of doing anything about it.

We have to do it.

In Langley, John and the others had reached the same conclusion as Rex.

Rex said, "You've got a serious problem, General. You might want to contact General Dai immediately, tell him what's going on, and prepare for tomorrow's meeting."

"Prepare for what? It's going to be a disaster."

"So far, you and Dai have managed to mislead Tao. Maybe the two of you can do the same with Li. Maybe you want to tell him you've changed your mind since Saturday?"

Lang was crestfallen. He sighed deeply. "I guess I don't have other options... unless I ask you to extract me out of China immediately... but that means it's all over. Tao will be president, and the country will be doomed. My people will be slaughtered."

Rex didn't reply; Lang had answered his own question. He only nodded. He had a plan, but it had to be discussed with Langley, and even if they approved, it had to be kept from Lang.

Five minutes later, Lang was on his way to see General Dai, and Rex was on his way to the hotel.

John told Howard, "Rex will have a plan. Don't ask me what, but take my word for it; he's got a plan. So, in order to save time, I suggest you contact the president and get his approval to let Rex and his team remove Li from the monastery."

Howard hesitated for a few moments, nodded, and picked up the phone. It took him about ten minutes to explain to the president what had happened and what had to be done to save the mission. It took the president less than thirty seconds to agree.

When Rex and Digger walked into the hotel room, Catia already had the secured video link to Langley established.

Rex said, "John, I have a plan. I hope you have the president's preapproval?"

"I would've been embarrassed if you didn't have a plan. Yes, we have preapproval. Now we only have to hear your plan."

Rex told them. His plan was simple, daring, and brilliant, and they approved.

But Rex didn't tell them that he was already working on the next plan, which would bring the presidential race to an abrupt end.

Howard whispered to Martin, "It's as if John and Rex can read each other's minds."

Martin smiled. "I think sometimes they can. But you should see him and Digger in action. It'll blow your mind away. I'm prepared to put my hand on the Bible and swear they speak a language which only they understand."

Chapter Forty

LET'S GET BACK TO BEIJING AND GO TO WORK

Tuesday morning, Guilin, China

The flight from Xijao military airport to Qifengling military airport near Guilin took a little over three hours in the small military passenger jet. Lang and Dai were worried. Even though they'd spent the whole night preparing for the meeting, they knew a lot could still go wrong, not the least of which was that Li would not believe Lang's about-face since seeing him a few days ago.

The helicopter ride to the monastery was only twenty minutes.

As usual on these visits, the pilot dropped the three men off and left immediately. No one came out to meet them. That was expected. Li and his concubine were under strict orders not to come out of the monastery during the daytime unless they were both in disguise lest the satellites saw their faces and recognized them.

What was unexpected, though, was the open front door

and no one to greet them. Dai went in first with Lang and Tao short on his heels.

Dai called out but got no reply.

They looked at each other, alarmed. But they were soldiers; they were not supposed to be scared. They began moving slowly through the place.

Ten minutes later, they were in agreement; Li Lingxin and his courtesan, Ding Cui, were not inside. There were no signs of a struggle. Apart from the missing occupants, the contents of a filing cabinet and Li's computers were also missing.

They expanded their search to the outside, even daring to venture into the jungle, but all for naught. There was no response to any of their calls. Neither had their abductors left any visual clues of where they came from nor where they went.

Dai's briefing by Lang didn't include anything about his collaboration with the CIA. So, at some stage, when they were not within sight of Tao, Dai looked at Lang with raised eyebrows as if to ask, "Do you know what's going on?" Lang only shrugged and shook his head.

Dai was somewhat relieved that they didn't have to deal with Li and Tao. However, fear outweighed the relief as his mind was bombarded with the far-reaching consequences of what he believed happened there.

Lang was sure he knew what had happened, but he had to pretend he was just as concerned as his companions.

Tao had his own emotional battle raging. Although it would have been helpful to have Li's support in his pursuit of the presidency, he wasn't dependent on it. Or was he? If whoever abducted them and took the computers knew who Li was, he and the entire cohort of Trustees were looking at life in prison or, more likely the firing squad.

After another hour of searching in vain, they were sitting in the living room having tea and tried, also in vain, to unravel what could have happened but, more importantly, what they could do about it. It wasn't as if they could call the police in to launch a manhunt for the former dead president.

"We're wasting time. Forget about finding them. The people who abducted them either knew who they are or are going to find out very soon. We have to think what we're going to do to save our own skins and our comrades who participated in this subterfuge."

"As far as I know, Liao doesn't know the secret. Does anyone of you know if that has changed?" Tao asked.

"When I met with him on Friday, he still didn't know," said Lang.

"Not as far as I know," said Dai.

An evil grin appeared on Tao's face. "Let's say Liao did know but hid it from you, then he could be behind this. He might use Li as leverage against the Trustees to make them vote for his plan."

Lang realized he had to get Tao off that train of thought very quickly. "Not impossible, but how to verify it without asking him directly? And if he didn't know about Li before, he would know when you ask him, and then you would've handed him the loaded gun to shoot us with."

Tao nodded, deep in thought. He got up to pour himself another cup of tea. When his back was turned, Lang caught Dai's eye and placed his finger on his lips in a be-quiet motion. Dai got the message and nodded once, imperceptibly.

Tao was back in his seat. "Okay, here's what I think. We go back and talk to each of the Trustees individually. Tell them what happened and that they are in danger irrespective of who is behind this. Whichever way this comes to light, the only way we're going to survive is if I'm president so that I can pardon us all."

Lang immediately detected the flaw in Tao's plan. If he can pardon, so can Liao. And Liao was already president; he could pardon people immediately. But he was not going to make Tao wise about that.

"Now that's a brilliant plan, Chairman. I suggest we get back to Beijing and go to work."

About one hundred and fifty miles north of the monastery, on a farm belonging to a member of the Tuidang Movement, the former President of the Republic of China and his courtesan were in the basement of the house in a medically induced coma.

Tuidang is short for Tuichu Gongchandang and translates literally as leave or quit the Party. The Chinese Communist Party (CCP), that is. They are a peaceful grassroots resistance movement established in 2004 and now numbering more than 300 million members and counting, who had renounced the oaths they had made to the Communist Party. According to their website, their mission is: To investigate and document the atrocities communism has perpetrated against humanity. To assist all ethnic Chinese worldwide to renounce communist indoctrination and culture. To provide a means for all ethnic Chinese to withdraw from the Chinese Communist Party, Young Pioneers, and the Communist Youth League. To help the Chinese people take their first steps toward individual liberty and help them adjust to living in a free society. And to coordinate the global Tuidang movement.

Some human-rights experts believed the movement had the ability to peacefully disintegrate the Chinese Communist Party. Lech Walesa, former Polish President, called them "History's Tsunami."

It was Tuidang members who helped Flat Arrow and his family escape from China about four months ago. And it was through Flat Arrow's contacts that Rex was able to get the 'temporary accommodation' for Li Lingxin and company on the farm. The owner had no idea who his 'guests' were.

Chapter Forty-One

HE GAVE HIS APPROVAL

Tuesday morning, Beijing, China

Rex and his team were back in Beijing by 9:00 a.m. after their overnight excursion to Guilin to abduct and hide the former President of the PRC. On the flight from Guilin in Jethro's private jet, they all slept from takeoff to landing. Rex had closed his eyes and tried to think through his plan for the next phase of the mission, but within minutes he gave up and surrendered to his body's appeals for sleep.

Lang was in a hurry to report to Badger and test his theory about who was responsible for the surprise at the monastery. He followed the protocol to get an urgent encoded message to him requesting a meeting for that evening.

Back at the hotel, after taking a shower with Catia and a three-hour nap in each other's arms, he got up very quietly so as not to wake her. He took a soft drink and snack out of the minibar and took Digger for a walk in a nearby park. It was time to discuss his plan with his best friend and mentor.

He found an empty and isolated bench, sat down, and said to Digger, "Okay, buddy, sit down and listen carefully. I have a plan to run by you."

Digger sat down and yawned. Rex interpreted that to mean, "I already know all about your plan." But it was also possible that he was stressed about something, and the yawn helped calm him down.

"Of course, you know. I keep forgetting you can read my mind. But would you mind if I lay it out for you? It will help me to get things straight."

Digger laid down but kept his eyes fixed on Rex as if to say, "Go for it, I'm all ears." Or maybe he sensed they were going to be there for a while and wanted to get a bit more comfortable.

Rex explained the entire plan, and Digger didn't interrupt him once. "So, what do you think?"

Digger yelped once.

"So you think it's great?"

Digger yelped again.

"Thanks, I thought you might like it." But maybe Digger's yelps were just him saying hi to the cute woolly Chow Chow and her owner, passing by.

"I think you should come along to meet the guy. What do you say?"

Digger made no reply.

"Not interested, really?" Rex leaned closer to Digger. "Come on, buddy, just think about it; how many dogs do you know who can say they rubbed shoulders with the presidents of America, China, and France? Besides, there could be another medal in it for you."

Digger licked him in the face, which, according to Rex, meant, "Well, if you put it that way. When can we go?" Or, maybe, Digger was just expressing his affection for his alpha.

Half an hour later, Rex and Digger were back at the hotel. He woke Catia, phoned the Farleys in their room, and asked them to come over. There was a lot to do before the meeting with Lang at 8:00 p.m.

Next, he sent an encrypted text message to John to get the usual crowd together in Langley for a video conference. The last few weeks, since Rex and his team had been operating out of Hong Kong, they had gotten used to meeting in the dead of night because of the twelve-hour time difference. It was 1:30 a.m. in Langley and 1:30 p.m. in Beijing when John received the message.

Forty-five minutes later, they were in conference with John, Christelle, Ollie, Howard, Martin, and Cupcake in the ops room in Langley. The Daltons and Farleys were on the Beijing side of the call. In Langley, Cupcake was in her usual corner with her kong full of beef jerky. She loved these meetings.

John said, "Okay, Dalton, the floor is yours."

Rex stepped them through his plan just like he did with Digger earlier in the park and Catia and the Farleys in the hotel room. The crowd in Langley was quiet. After the greetings, Digger had retreated to the couch with his kong filled with peanut butter. He had heard the plan twice already and approved it twice. He had nothing to add.

Rex's plan was unorthodox, but that was often the case with his plans, and thus far, they'd always worked out. Everyone liked the idea that Rex's plan could bring a swift end to the idiocy of Chairman Tao and his supporters so that the negotiations could start.

Rex was smiling when he came to the end. "Over to

you, John. Just keep in mind I ran it past Digger earlier, and he gave his approval."

Howard did a double-take when he heard that. He glanced at Martin and found him smiling from ear to ear. "I told you he and the dog talk to each other." Nevertheless, with his background in the diplomatic service, Howard immediately saw the merit of Rex's plan. Even so, the plan required presidential approval. He was on the phone with the president shortly after. It took him less than ten minutes to get the necessary approval.

Chapter Forty-Two

KEEPS HIS SHOES ON AT ALL TIMES

Tuesday evening, Beijing, China

By 8:00 p.m., just like the night before, Rex and Digger were back in Lin's living room with General Lang.

Rex listened intently to Lang describing what had happened at the monastery near Guilin earlier in the day.

While talking, Lang tried his level best to detect any signs that Badger had prior knowledge. But he never had a chance; Rex was highly skilled in avoiding lie detectors of both the human and electronic kind. The only lie detector he would be unable to dupe was fast asleep on the carpet next to his chair.

Finding no signs of duplicity in Rex's demeanor, Lang tried the direct approach. "You don't perchance happen to know who abducted Li and his wife?"

Rex laughed out loud. "No, General, I don't."

When Lang finished, Rex said, "So, what do you think of Tao's idea to offer the marshals a blank pardon in exchange for their votes?"

"It can work, but Liao can offer them the same deal. And the fact that he is the president right now enables him to issue pardons preemptively."

"Good point. But that means you'll have to inform him about Li. What do you think will be his reaction when he finds out about your involvement in the entire affair? Especially since you didn't inform him when you joined forces with him a few days ago."

"I anticipate that he might not be happy. But he is a pragmatic man. He will get over it quickly and focus on getting the support of the rest of the marshals."

"Okay, sounds good, but what are you and Liao telling your countrymen and the world when the news is released that the marshals deliberately misled them for the past year?"

Lang shrugged. "I've been thinking about that, but I don't have an answer. I think that's something Liao is better equipped to deal with if it comes to that. Your president and the CIA already know. Have you got any advice for us?"

"It's quite possible, but I wouldn't know. All I can tell you is that I've been instructed to make arrangements through you for an urgent meeting between President Liao and our ambassador here in Beijing. But I don't know what's going to be on the agenda."

Lang leaned forward. "How soon?"

"Tonight."

"I'll get right on it."

Rex held his hand up. "Before you go, here are the conditions: The ambassador will be accompanied by a special envoy from the President of the United States. President Liao will be alone. In other words, there will be only three people in the room. There will be no translators, no eavesdropping, and no recordings of any kind whatsoever. If that's acceptable to President Liao, text me the time. The ambassador and the envoy are standing by to leave for Zhongnanhai the moment he gets the time."

Lang agreed to convey the request and conditions and left.

Rex rushed back to the hotel. The meeting was scheduled for 11:30 p.m. He told them that although they'd picked the right sizes for his entire outfit except for maybe the shoes, he still felt like a fish out of water. But they had little sympathy with him.

"Digger, please make sure caveman Badger here keeps his shoes on at all times when you're in the president's house," were Josh's parting shot as Rex and Digger left the room to meet ambassador Adrien Gillis in front of the hotel.

Chapter Forty-Three

THEN HE AND THE GENERAL WENT TO WORK

Tuesday evening, Zhongnanhai, Beijing, China

It's not unusual for world leaders to meet in complete privacy, with no interpreters, officials, or aides present. The meeting tonight was one of those and would take place in the president's private study at Zhongnanhai. The president's Chief of Security and three of his men, all members of the Central Security Bureau (CSB), responsible for the security of senior government officials, would be on duty outside the room for the duration.

Even though Gillis had been fully briefed by Howard Lawrence and Lauren Woods, the Secretary of State, Rex would do most of the talking.

Gillis's and Rex's arrival was expected. As per the president's instructions, they were met at the security gate by the Chief of Security in person. They were scanned and requested to leave their mobile phones and other electronic devices at the security checkpoint. The Security Chief had no comments about Digger's presence. If he objected, Gillis would've told him Digger was a service dog who had to accompany Mr. James Neilsen, the US president's special envoy, at all times. Mr. Neilsen had a doctor's letter to confirm it if so required.

Digger snarled when the CSB agent approached him with a handheld scanner. The agent stopped in his tracks and looked at the Chief of Security for instructions. The chief waved for him to let it go, and Digger relaxed. Even if he did scan Digger, he would have discovered nothing strange, not even the mini microphones in the collar's shiny metallic studs or the micro recorder in the buckle. They were all switched off.

None of them believed for one moment that President Liao wouldn't have recording devices hidden somewhere in the study. But it would have been atrocious manners to insist on sweeping the room for bugs. Hence, the solution was to smuggle their own devices in to avoid disputes about what was said.

Ambassador Gillis and President Liao knew each other quite well. When the president shook hands with Rex, Digger sat down next to him and extended his right paw. President Liao frowned when he saw it. Rex explained that Digger was harmless and, like all dogs, loved to show off to get attention.

Liao laughed, bent down, and shook Digger's proffered paw. "Pleased to meet you, Mr. Digger."

Rex was smiling when he stooped and ruffled Digger's ears, "Good boy." The smiling was not so much about the humor in the situation as the fact that Digger sensed no malice in Liao. He would never offer to shake paws with a human he didn't trust. It was a good start. And the eaves-dropping equipment on Digger's collar was now active.

There was a table to the side loaded with refreshments

to which Liao led them first and invited them to help themselves.

A few minutes later, they were seated, and Liao started. "Mr. Ambassador, I'm ready to hear what's on your mind."

"Thank you, Mr. President. One of the reasons for this visit is to discuss arrangements for the private meeting between you and our president. But I suggest we leave that for last. Mr. Neilsen has some more pressing matters to discuss first."

Rex could hear Liao taking a deep breath as if bracing himself for bad news. There was no reason to beat around the bush. So Rex gave it to him straight, warts and all. He told him that Li Lingxin was not dead. That he and the rest of the country had been the victims of a fraudulent scheme created by the ten marshals known as the Trustees, who, as he knew, was chaired by his current righthand man, General Lang Jianhong.

They spent several minutes discussing that shocking revelation before Rex continued and administered the next shock. Li and his courtesan had been abducted the night before.

When Rex told him that the Chairman of the Central Military Commission, Tao Huan, was planning to bribe the marshals with the promise of presidential pardons if they made him president, Liao grinned, almost as if he was thanking Tao for the idea.

By now, President Liao must have figured out that Mr. Neilsen must either be General Lang's CIA handler or be in close contact with the handler. Nevertheless, he neither mentioned it nor enquired who Mr. Neilsen's source was.

He also didn't enquire if Mr. Neilsen might have any idea who could've abducted Li Lingxin and his courtesan and their possible whereabouts. Maybe he knew if the

Americans had them, they'd never admit it—definitely not at this stage. Or, maybe he didn't suspect the Americans at all.

———

This time Rex's team and John et al. in Langley had no idea what was happening in the meeting. They had to wait until Rex returned with the recording. They were used to having ringside seats at these Rex Dalton shows. It was utterly frustrating to be excluded, not to mention nerve-wracking.

John was like a father whose daughter was out on her prom night waiting for her to come home. First, he started pacing in the meeting room but got kicked out by Christelle. Then he took to pacing around the open office until Ollie turned up in his wheelchair with Cupcake on a leash.

"John, the boy is going to be okay. You've seen him in action the last few days. The kid's got more talent and skill than the two of us combined, on our best days."

"Yeah, I guess you're right. I've known him for almost seventeen years now. He's the best field agent I've ever seen, period. But I had no idea how good he was going to be at this spy stuff."

"Exactly. Now, let's take Madame Cupcake for a walk."

———

In the meantime, in President Liao's private study, the discussions had moved on from the shocking news sections to the pragmatic section; how to use that information to end the reign of the marshals once and for all so that the peace talks could commence.

Again Mr. Neilsen displayed remarkable insight about

and intimate knowledge of the battle for the presidency that had been raging behind the scenes since President Liao's shock announcement at the Trustees meeting five days ago. Yet, the president made no mention of it, even if it was evident that not only must Mr. Neilsen have had access to the transcript of that fateful meeting but also to what had been said in secret meetings afterward.

It was 2:40 a.m. when Rex summarized the plan of action, and the meeting ended.

Fifteen minutes later, the Peregrine team was listening to the recording which Rex had retrieved from the buckle of Digger's collar.

It was about the same time when General Lang stepped into President Liao's private study. The first ten minutes or so, the general got an ass-chewing the likes of which he last had when he was a private.

Liao showed him pictures of Mr. Neilsen and his dog, captured by the CCTV cameras when he and the ambassador passed through the security checkpoint upon arrival and departure. Lang didn't recognize Mr. Neilsen but had little doubt that the big black dog belonged to the man he knew as Badger, his CIA handler.

Liao shrugged. "Okay, let's not dwell on the real identity of Mr. Neilsen; it's of academic value now. We've got a lot of work to do before sunrise."

Chapter Forty-Four

BUT THEN EVERYTHING CHANGED

Wednesday late afternoon, Beijing, China

It was shortly after 4:00 a.m. when General Jin Ping's phone rang. When he heard the voice of President Liao, he almost had an embarrassing accident in his pajama pants.

He arrived at Zhongnanhai less than an hour later to receive his orders.

The first part of his orders he executed within half an hour after arriving at his office located in the Underground Great Wall of China. The second part he would execute as soon as General Xia Wei, in command of Operation Middle Kingdom, arrived at his office in the same underground complex.

China has another great wall. At 3,000 miles, this wall is not known to many; in fact, the authorities keep its existence a secret. It is known as the Underground Great Wall of China, consisting of a labyrinth of tunnels used by the PRC to store and transport mobile intercontinental ballistic missiles. Western intelligence sources don't know much about the tunnels but have obtained information indicating that the tunnels were reinforced with a special type of steel invented by Chinese scientists that would withstand attacks by bunker-buster bombs and nuclear weapons.

It was inside one of these underground facilities on the outskirts of Beijing where General Jin Ping's office was located, and several divisions of special cyberespionage units toiled 24/7.

By 5:00 a.m. Shen Delan had received his instructions from the president and hurried to his office to do as ordered. He had to put tabs on seven marshals of the PLA whom the president and General Lang had reason to believe were conspiring to remove Liao from office. Precisely how and when they were planning to do it was his job to find out.

Chairman Tao Huan was up at 6:00 a.m. He was going to work from home today. While having breakfast, he checked his email. The most important among the emails that came in overnight was the one notifying the Trustees that the Thursday meeting had been brought forward to tonight at 7:00 p.m. Lang didn't give the reason for the change, but Tao didn't mind.

"Suits me fine. If Liao wants to vacate his office a day earlier, I'm not going to stop him."

The day before, on the plane back from Guilin, Tao got a solid undertaking from Lang and Dai that they would inform Wan Huang, Jin Ping, Xia Wei, Zeng Jiahao, and Wu Shuren about the problems facing them now that Li has disappeared and offer them the way out as he had suggested.

His mission today was to get Deng Jie, Shao Yong, and Kong Yuhan aboard. He didn't foresee too much trouble with that. It was not as if they had many options; it was a take it or spend the rest of your life in jail kind of proposition.

General Xia arrived at his office at 7:45 a.m. Jin walked in a few minutes later and invited him for breakfast. Over breakfast, Jin explained what a grim future awaited all of them if Liao didn't remain in the saddle. For Tao had announced, to him, Jin, in confidence, he would use this opportunity to get the marshals out of the way. Of course, that bit was a lie, but Xia wouldn't know.

"Be aware, Tao might contact you during the day. If he does, please meet with him but don't believe a word he says. When I spoke to him yesterday, he was quite adamant that he holds you solely responsible for the failed Malacca Strait and Taiwan missions. He even hinted that you might be the source of the leak about Li Lingxin and his whereabouts to those who abducted him."

By the time the breakfast was over, Jin had instilled the fear of God in Xia. Tao Huan didn't have a prayer that would get him Xia's support.

By 8:00 a.m. Tao started phoning the marshals on his list.

Deng Jie's phone went straight to voicemail, *probably in a meeting,* he left a message. He would have been horrified to know that Deng never got that message, and at that moment, Deng was with Liao and had just reaffirmed his support for the president and made a promise to ensure that Shao Yong followed his lead.

Shao Yong's phone didn't ring at all, *probably in an area*

with no reception. He sent him a text message and email, which he would get as soon as he had reception again. Tao didn't know that Shao was not going to get the messages until an hour after he had met with Admiral Deng Jie.

Kong Yuhan answered, but the phone cut out immediately after. Tao tried again and got the same result; he sent a text message but got no response. *His phone must be defective.* He sent an email hoping Kong's computer was still functional.

If Tao knew what Jin Ping had been up to since his early morning meeting with President Liao, he wouldn't have bothered making phone calls or sending text messages or emails to any of them. But as it were, he didn't know and relied on the technology that Jin had sabotaged.

By 11:00 a.m. Tao was a little nervous as the clock was ticking away relentlessly. He knew he had seven votes in the bag among the Trustees, enough to stop Liao tonight. But he wanted to end it tonight. Liao had to go tonight and not a moment later.

He started phoning the seven marshals who were not Trustees. He managed to get hold of them fairly easily and told them that the big day had been brought forward by 24 hours. They had to gather at his house at 5:30 p.m. to finalize the plans for tonight.

If Tao had known that his every move and every telephone call were being monitored and recorded by the MSS and that they had the same surveillance in place for the seven marshals, he would have gotten on the first flight out of China and found himself a country where he could live the rest of his life in anonymity.

By 4:00 p.m., he had confirmation from Lang and Dai that he had the support of Wan Huang, Jin Ping, Xia Wei,

Zeng Jiahao, and Wu Shuren. He had personally met with Deng and Shao Yong, and they brought the tally to nine.

At 4:30 p.m., he finally received a call from Kong.

"My apologies, Chairman, I had a day from hell with technology today. I'll come over immediately." He was at Tao's house in less than fifteen minutes. The meeting lasted ten minutes, and Tao had the support of all seventeen marshals.

By 5:25 p.m., the seven marshals started arriving. By 5:30 p.m., all of them were gathered in Tao's spacious and opulent study. The CSB agents responsible for Tao's security were given photos of the marshals and told to identify them on arrival and not harass them with the usual search routines.

If the agents had been allowed to do their jobs and conducted full-body scans, they would have found nothing suspicious. But if they were to take every visitor's mobile phone and conducted a forensic audit on the devices, they would have discovered that three of the phones had non-standard applications installed on them, which turned those phones into something akin to radio stations. The owners of those phones, just like the CSB agents, had no idea.

By 6:15 p.m., Tao was getting antsy; it would take at least half an hour to get to Zhongnanhai. The plan was in place; the seven marshals were in full support. They would make their way to Zhongnanhai and wait close by for Tao's call.

Tao was on his feet, ready to go, but then everything changed.

Chapter Forty-Five

TO THE HOLDING CELLS

Wednesday evening, Beijing, China

First, they heard the unmistakable thumping sound of helicopters approaching, then they heard loud voices coming from above and knew they were in serious trouble.

None of them were armed; generals dressed in tunics didn't carry guns. Their security guards did, but they didn't fire a single shot. The guards would have had to have death wishes to shoot at the MSS agents—none of them had such a wish.

By 6:20 p.m., a stern-faced Minister Shen Delan exited the helicopter that had landed on the lawn in front of Tao's house. Accompanied by six heavily armed and body-armored MSS agents, he entered the house and proceeded to the study, where they found a red-faced Chairman Tao and seven highly irritated marshals.

As expected, a brouhaha ensued. What's the meaning of this? Have you lost your mind? Do you have any idea how much trouble you're in?

But Minister Shen had been listening to every word that was said in the meeting and had no doubts; the attendees were guilty of a whole raft of very serious crimes, including conspiracy to overthrow the government, high treason, sedition, subversion, mutiny, rebellion, and probably a few others.

Under heavy protests and threats of the unspeakable fate that awaited Shen Delan and his men when they were released, which they assured him, would be within the hour, Shen ignored it all and ordered his men to handcuff the eight conspirators and transport them to the MSS's holding cells for questioning.

Promises fulfilled

Wednesday evening, Zhongnanhai, Beijing, China

The trustees meeting started right on time at 7:00 p.m. Upon arrival at the meeting room, everyone was scanned and searched by the president's CSB agents. They were relieved of their mobile phones, briefcases, and watches. On the oval conference table were microphones on stands in front of each attendee. In the corner was a video camera.

It was to be their last meeting; they all knew that. What they didn't know was why Chairman Tao was not there.

Instead of Lang starting the meeting, as usual, Liao did. "I've made promises to you; I will keep them. You've made promises to me, and I'm sure you'll keep them. Half an hour ago, Chairman Tao and seven marshals were arrested by agents of the MSS on charges of conspiracy to overthrow the government, high treason, subversion, and others. Chairman Tao will not be attending the meeting tonight."

It would've been possible to hear a pin drop on the carpet as the marshals processed what they'd heard. The era of marshal rule was over. They were relieved for various reasons, but mostly that all their transgressions would be forgiven. They would not meet with the same fate as their seven colleagues currently in the MSS cells.

"What happens if Li Lingxin... how can I put it... makes an appearance?" General Xia asked.

"He might show up someday or never. I will deal with it if and when it's necessary," replied Liao.

There were no more questions.

Liao continued. "The first promise I made to you was that you won't be arrested or charged. I've now delivered on that.

"In exchange, you've all promised to bring your signed letters of resignation with you. And I've promised to swap each of those for a presidential pardon. I have ten of them here, signed and dated. Let's do it."

One by one, the marshals stood, approached President Liao, handed him their letters, took delivery of their pardons, and left the room.

Lang was last in line. That was the end of the meeting and the end of Chairman Tao and the Trustees. The matter of Li Lingxin remained unresolved.

Nevertheless, China was not going to war.

A technician came in, removed the videotape, and handed it to the president.

Lang accompanied Liao to his office. "I don't accept your resignation," said Liao when they were in the safety of his office. "I am going to recommend that you be the temporary Chairman of the Central Military Commission until the Politburo appoints a new one.

"After that, you will be my new Chief of Staff. The current Chief of Staff had been spying on me on behalf of Tao.

"Oh, and before I forget, you will note that your pardon is missing a date and my signature."

Lang needed no explanation. It was abundantly clear, he was given a second chance, but he'd have to stay on the straight and narrow from here on in. He thanked the president, bid him a good night, and left.

It was 8:00 p.m. when Liao was put through to Ambassador Gillis and asked him if he would be so kind as to come over to Zhongnanhai immediately.

Gillis was there within the hour.

President Liao thanked the ambassador for responding so promptly. He told Gillis that the marshals were not a problem anymore and that the negotiations could begin. He handed Gillis an envelope containing a copy of the video-tape made during the Trustees' final meeting earlier. With that, Liao had fulfilled his promise to the ambassador the night before.

Gillis thanked him and told him that he would transfer the contents of the tape to Washington electronically as soon as he was back at the embassy. And that President Liao could expect a call from the President of the United States within the next twelve hours. And that would be Gillis's fulfillment of his promise to President Liao the night before.

President Liao also had a message for Mr. Neilsen. "I'm pretty sure that's not his real name. It doesn't matter, though. That man with the big black dog made a momentous contribution to help us avoid a cataclysmic war between our countries."

"I couldn't say it better myself, Mr. President."

Liao handed Gillis another envelope. "Just a personal thank-you note for Mr. Neilsen. I'd appreciate it if you could give it to him."

"It'd be my pleasure, sir."

"Thank you again for meeting on such short notice, Mr. Ambassador. I'm looking forward to the call from your president."

Chapter Forty-Six

A PERSONAL LETTER

Wednesday night, Beijing, China

When Gillis arrived back at the embassy, Rex was waiting for him. First, they encrypted the video and uploaded it to the Peregrine servers. Then he gave Rex a recount of the meeting with Liao. They watched the video recording of the meeting, and Gillis handed him the letter from President Liao.

Back at the hotel, he and Catia invited the Farleys over to their room, and Rex read the president's letter for them.

Just like the letter to the President of the United States a few days before, this letter was also in black ink, in his own elegant handwriting, on the president's official stationery. And in a similar fashion to the previous letter, short and to the point.

Dear Mr. Neilsen,
  My country and I will be eternally grateful for your contribution

to enable our respective nations to head for a negotiation table rather than a war.

I am sure Ambassador Gillis would have informed you of the outcome of the final meeting of the Trustees. An outcome that you helped us accomplish. The only outstanding matter from that meeting is the whereabouts of the man who started it all. Any assistance you can give us to find him would be much appreciated.

Sincerely yours,

Liao Qigang

President of the People's Republic of China

Rex took a photo of the letter on his mobile phone and emailed it to John.

"I usually struggle to read between the lines of politician-speak, but I get the feeling this guy is pretty sure you know where their ex is," said Josh.

"Yep. I saw the video of tonight's meeting. Xia asked Liao directly what's going to happen if Li turns up somewhere. Liao brushed it off saying, he'll deal with it if and when it happens. He didn't seem worried about it."

"I know it's not our decision to make, but what would you do?" said Marissa.

"I'd hand him over in a heartbeat," said Rex.

"They'll kill him," said Catia.

"You want to keep the ratbag alive?" Josh asked.

"Absolutely. I want him sent to one of those Uyghur reeducation camps for starters."

"I'll support that," said Marissa. "I hope they make him the toilet cleaner in chief."

They had their answer

Washington D.C., USA

While the four in Beijing were considering an appropriate punishment for Li Lingxin, in Washington, the President of the United States was in conclave with the members of the Cold War Council.

They were relieved that the first hurdle had been crossed. It was a nail-biter from start to finish. But apart from the fact that it opened the doors to the peace talks, it also helped establish bonafides on both sides—always a good departure point for any negotiations.

The president would phone President Liao as soon as this meeting ended.

The final matter to consider was what to do about Li Lingxin. They were still debating the pros and cons of each option when Howard received a text message from John with a copy of Rex's letter attached. He read it out loud.

They had their answer. President Liao will deal with Li Lingxin.

"I wish I could get a personal message to that son of a bitch," grumbled the president, "but I guess this will have to do."

Ten minutes later, Rex had received orders from John to move Li and his courtesan back to the monastery and let Lang know where to find him.

Chapter Forty-Seven

A FEW FAVORS

Thursday night, Beijing, China

By nightfall, Rex was on his final errand in Beijing, giving General Lang some last-minute advice before he and the team would return to the USA.

"Congratulations, General. My understanding is that the miracle you so desperately needed has indeed happened."

"It did indeed, and if not for your wise counsel, it would never have happened."

"I'm glad we could be of service. What are your plans for the future now that you don't need to relocate to America?"

Lang told him about the temporary Chairman of the Central Military Commission role and then taking over as Chief of Staff.

"Congratulations again. I take it you're happy with that outcome?"

"I am. I take it our relationship is at an end now?"

"If you want it to be, but look at what we've achieved by cooperating. Why would you want to end it? Let's stay in touch."

"Well... when you put it like that, it doesn't sound like spying anymore. I can live with that."

"Excellent. Now, I was hoping you could do me a few favors?"

"Name it."

"What is your driver's name?"

Lang shook his head. "I'm sorry, but I don't know. Why?"

"His name is Corporal Adil Tursun. He's fifty-seven. He's the son of a dirt-poor Uyghur peasant family from the Xinjiang area. He's an intelligent, diligent, and loyal man, but he has been discriminated against based on his ethnicity his entire life in the military. He has more than thirty-five years of service, his record is clean, but he has had only two promotions. Do you think that's fair, General?"

Lang was embarrassed. He was shaking his head. "No, it's not."

"So that's the favor I want to ask you. Please remember his name. Please give him the promotions he was supposed to have had with full backpay and promote him to be one of the president's drivers."

Lang nodded slowly. "You have my word. Before the sun sets tomorrow, those injustices will be rectified, and he will be one of the president's drivers."

"Much appreciated. Oh, just so you know, I have never met Corporal Tursun. He is not spying for us."

"I believe you."

"The next favor is about your *aide-de-camp*, Colonel Dong Qui. He and one of your guards murdered an old, uneducated, innocent, and defenseless Christian lady. Do you think it's fair that they should go unpunished even though they are working for you?"

Lang was quiet. He shook his head slowly and whispered, "No, it's not."

"And that's the last favor I want to ask you. Here's the name and address of a Catholic Church not far from Dong's house." Rex handed him a piece of paper. "I want Dong and the guard to report to the parish priest and offer their services to do charity work among the poor. No less than ten hours per week, and they *will* attend the Sunday morning mass every week without exception for the next ten years or until they die, whichever comes first. The priest's name and telephone number are on there. He is waiting for their call."

"I will make sure it happens. And I have to say I'm stunned by your altruism. Admittedly, it's something I have a lot to learn about."

Rex thanked the general for his help and cooperation and stood to leave. Then he stopped in the middle of a sentence and bumped his forehead with an open palm. "I almost forgot to tell you. I've heard a rumor that Li Lingxin has decided to move back into the monastery."

Lang stared at him for a long while with a neutral expression, and then he started laughing. "One day, you'll have to tell me who you really are, Mr. Badger."

Rex smiled. "I won't be able to. Not because I am not allowed to but because I deliberately keep myself in a state of utter confusion—not even I know who I am."

Lang was roaring with laughter.

In Langley, Ollie said to John, "That boy of yours is full of pleasant surprises."

"Yep, that's Rex Dalton for you."

Epilogue

THEIR LIVES WERE ABOUT TO CHANGE

Friday morning, Guilin, China

When Li and Ding Cui awoke from the coma early on Friday morning, they were in the same bed and bedroom that they were in when they went to sleep. But both had a strange feeling that they didn't wake up from a typical night's sleep. They discovered they were right when they switched on the TV and learned with a shock that they'd been asleep for almost three days.

They had no knowledge of the helicopter carrying four dark-clad humans and a big black dog dropping them off at 3:15 a.m., two miles from their home, on Tuesday.

Neither did they know that the humans and the dog had entered their home and sedated them. They had no knowledge that they had been transported to a farm one hundred and fifty miles away from the monastery where they were kept until about six hours ago when they were transported back and placed in their bed.

Adding to their disorientation was the discovery that the computers and files in the filing cabinet were missing, and Li's satellite phone was also nowhere to be found.

About fifteen minutes after they woke up, Li and Ding were relieved to hear the sound of an approaching helicopter. But within a few minutes after welcoming Generals Lang Jianhong and Dai Min, Li knew that his and Ding's lives were about to change, and it was highly unlikely to be for the better.

About democracy

Friday night, Manhattan, New York

Senator Jordyn Lancaster had been looking forward to this dinner for months. She had deliberately selected the same classy restaurant in Manhattan where, about five months ago, Song Yuhan introduced himself to her as the Chinese Cultural attaché stationed in New York. But in truth, he was a Chinese spy, and thanks to the FBI, Senator Lancaster was prepared for it.

As with their previous meetings, she gave Song a small USB flash drive containing classified information about foreign policy legislation currently being debated in her committee. She also told him that she was about to make a big breakthrough to get insider information from the House Intelligence Committee through a very senior committee member.

This brought a big smile to Song's face.

They were about to order dessert when the senator spotted two people she knew entering the restaurant. She waved at them, and they came over to her table. She stood when they arrived, shook hands with them, asked how they were doing, and asked if they'd like to sit down for a few minutes.

They accepted.

The look on Song's face made it clear he was not happy about that. She ignored him, looked at her friends, and said, "Where are my manners? I'm so sorry. This is Song Yuhan. He says he's a cultural attaché working out of the Cultural Office here in New York. But that's a lie; he's a spy. He works for the Chinese Ministry of State Security. He has been trying to blackmail me for months now—"

Song was on his feet. He was red in the face; his body shook with rage.

Lancaster said, "What's wrong, Yuhan? Don't leave now. I'd like to introduce you to my friends Lydia Andrews and Ellis Sherman. They're FBI Senior Special Agents working for the counter-espionage unit, and they've been begging me to meet you tonight."

As if on cue, the FBI agents produced their badges and placed them on the table for Song to inspect.

But he didn't even glance at the badges. His face was a combination of indignation, disbelief, and fear as he stared at Senator Lancaster, and the realization dawned that he had been made a fool of. Not only that, he was about to be arrested. "I'm going to leave right now."

Sherman raised his hand slowly in a stop motion and spoke softly and calmly. "Mr. Song, I suggest you sit down. Unless, of course, you prefer that we arrest and handcuff you here in front of all these people."

Song sunk back into his chair. He looked at Lancaster with hate-filled eyes. "You've been... you... those tapes are going to be released... you're... done. Destroyed. The end of your political ambitions."

"We'll have to see about that, Yuhan. I'm not too fussed about those tapes. Well, not nearly as much as you are."

"But... you hate the president... how could you?"

"Song, you've got a lot to learn about democracy. We allow people to disagree with each other. We even encourage it. The fact that I don't like the president doesn't mean I'm not a patriot. People are not traitors and rebels and a danger to society because they have different political views. We don't lock people up or send them to concentration camps for disagreeing with the government."

Song Yuhan was deported from the USA a week later and told to stay away—in perpetuity.

Six months later, Senator Lancaster announced that she was going to retire from politics at the end of her current term because she wanted to devote her time to the development of the film industry in Australia.

He was also smiling

Saturday evening, White House, Washington, D.C.

On the flight back from Beijing, Rex and the team got a call from Howard Lawrence. He informed them that the five of them, even Digger, plus John and Christelle (Cupcake was not mentioned), were invited to a private dinner with the First Family at the White House on Saturday night.

As can be expected, they were honored and accepted. And they were excited; Marissa, Catia, and Christelle visibly more so than Rex, Josh, and John. The women immediately started fretting about what to wear. Rex already had a suit, the one he wore when he met with President Liao. Josh had to get a suit quickly. Digger only needed grooming. He only smiled when asked how he felt about having dinner with the President of the United States and his wife. As if to say, "I don't know what all the fuss is about. We've all met the guy before."

The dinner was in the residence, also known as the executive mansion, where an executive chef, a sous chef, a kitchen steward, and two pastry team members were responsible for breakfast, lunch, and dinner for the first family and guests.

It was obvious that the first couple were well versed in the art of making nervous visitors feel at ease. Within minutes, their guests were laughing and talking as if they were old acquaintances. For the next two hours, until the last dish was served, they talked about everything from family and history to sports and science, but not a single word about politics—national or international.

Digger got a lot of attention from everyone, and he made no secret of the fact that of all the new people he'd met in this place, the chefs were his favorites.

Only when the after-dinner fruit and cheese platter with port wine had been served the president steered the conversation to the world's biggest headache—China.

He was smiling. "Are you all familiar with the expression 'there's no such thing as a free dinner?'"

Everyone was.

"Good. Because it's true." He must have noticed the worried looks on their faces. "Relax, I am not going to raise your taxes. I just want to hear your opinions about China. I have lots of advisors, good people, highly qualified, and much experienced, but none have been inside the belly of the beast like you've been.

"As you know, President Liao and I had our private powwow and agreed on the agenda for the first meeting of the negotiations. The negotiations can't fail. If they do, we're looking at a global catastrophe, the likes of which humanity has never seen. However, humanity has the means to avert this disaster, but make no mistake, it's going to require an international undertaking of immense proportions, not to mention unprecedented cooperation."

The president paused for a few beats. "Okay, I promise I'm now going to shut up and listen to you. So, here's my first question: What are the things I should worry about most?"

There was an awkward silence where everyone was waiting for someone else to speak first.

"Mr. President, I'd say it's all about trust," said John. "The Russian proverb *Doveryai, no proveryai*, which became Ronald Reagan's signature phrase *trust but verify*, comes to mind. Can you trust Liao or his successor to honor his undertakings once China has the food they need?"

"Speaking of Russia," said Christelle, "I suggest, Mr. President, that it would be prudent to keep an eye on them. They might see this as an opportunity to annex Ukraine and the Baltic states Estonia, Latvia, Lithuania, and Finland while the world's focus is on China."

"Mr. President, we don't know how much support President Liao has in the Politburo," said Josh. "My worry is a resurgence of the marshals or other military leaders. The assassination of President Liao, even just removing him from office, could have a detrimental impact on the negotiations."

"Sage advice," said the president as he nodded slowly, contemplatively. "Second question. How do I get the world to cooperate and not see this as an opportunity to exploit the situation for their own gain?"

Catia, Josh, and Marissa turned their heads to Rex. On the plane back from Beijing, they had a very similar conversation, and Rex had what they thought to be a brilliant idea.

"Mr. President, there are more than two-point-three billion Christians in the world. They make up more than thirty-one percent of the seven-point-six billion people on earth. The Christians are spread across the world very much like the Jews are. As a group, they could have a tremendous influence on their governments—"

"Yes, they could," interjected the president, "but then you'll have to overcome the interdenominational differences. I've read or heard somewhere there are more than forty-five thousand Christian denominations. It would be impossible to get them to work together."

"Mr. President, broadly speaking, there are only three Christian groups in the world: Roman Catholic, about one-point-three billion. Protestant, about eight hundred million. Orthodox, about two hundred and sixty million, of which about forty percent live in Russia. By definition, a Christian is someone who loves Jesus and who loves their neighbor as themselves. Those are common among all Christian denominations."

The president nodded.

Rex continued. "The Pope is the leader of roughly the same number of people as the entire population of China. Ask him to issue a global challenge to every Christian leader and every political leader who claims to be Christian, irrespective of denomination, to forget their differences for once and come together to help rescue their brothers and sisters in China."

Now the president wasn't only nodding; he was also smiling.

Even paradise has shadows...

Fact and Fiction

All the characters in the story come from my imagination. As I have said in the foreword, any likeness to actual people, alive or dead, businesses, companies, events, or places is entirely coincidental.

The *Colletotrichum* fungus described in the story exists, and it behaves as described. In other words, it can be dormant in the soil and decaying plant matter, even equipment, for many years. During those periods of dormancy, it is immune against treatments. However, when the fungus eventually becomes active, it enters the stomata, or 'air vents' of the plant and starts multiplying. In the early stages, the infection is invisible to the farmer. But when it has built up enough numbers, it switches from an unwanted parasite to a wholesale destroyer, demolishing the structural supports and cells of the plant.

However, the *Colletotrichum sublineolum* fungus only attacks sorghum plants. I've given my imagination a bit of free reign when I said it attacked all grains.

The statistics about starvation make for some somber

reading: 9 million people die every year of hunger and hunger-related diseases. That's more than 24,000 people per day, more than the combined death toll from AIDS, malaria, and tuberculosis. A child dies from hunger every 10 seconds, and every day 1 in 9 people go to bed hungry.

The information about the Great Chinese Famine of 1959 to 1961 is factually correct. The famine was caused by a combination of bad agricultural policies, economic mismanagement, and natural disasters such as droughts and floods in farming regions. A Chinese journalist Yang Jisheng wrote that there were 36 million deaths due to starvation, while another 40 million others failed to be born.

The shortage of arable land in China is a fact. And that is further hampered by poor regulation and bad farming practices, which have caused significant environmental damage. Widespread soil contamination has rendered 8 million acres of agricultural land unusable. It is indeed true that the Chinese population, 22 percent of the world's population, has only 7 percent of the world's arable land and 6 percent of its freshwater.

The information about the counterfeit money in circulation around the globe and the North Korean Superdollars is factually correct to the best of my knowledge.

The information about China hoarding gold is correct. In 2009 they had 1,054 tons of gold in reserve. By 2015 they had 1,658 tons, and by 2020 they had 1,948 tons in reserve. Experts believe that they are accumulating it to back the yuan as the new world currency instead of the US dollar.

The disguising techniques used by Rex throughout the story are not wishful thinking. CIA disguising experts can disguise people to rival what we have seen in Tom Cruise's

Mission Impossible movies. For example, during the presidency of George H.W. Bush, the CIA's chief of disguise entered the White House wearing a mask that was an exact replica of the face of a female colleague of hers. She sat in the intelligence briefing close to the president for the duration. When the meeting was over, she removed the disguise and surprised the president with the fact that he had been in the presence of an impersonator without an inkling of an idea.

The molar mics used by Rex and his team for communication throughout this story are real. More information is available on Sonitus Technologies' website.

Visitors to Hong Kong would not find Matz Island, nor would they find the Matz Enterprises building in the financial district or anywhere else. Likewise, a search of the records of the company registrar's offices for HK Securities or Matz Enterprises would come up empty.

To the best of my knowledge, the parts regarding the history of Jews of Hong Kong and Shanghai are correct.

The description which Josh gave about the Badger and how it collects honey is weird but true. As the name suggests, the Honey Badger loves honey, and when it finds a beehive, it emits malodorous, suffocating secretions from its anal glands, which causes the bees to flee while he scoops out the honeycombs.

The information about the Underground Great Wall of China contained in this story is, to the best of my knowledge, accurate. So is the existence of Unit 61398, a division of the People's Liberation Army (PLA), the alleged source of Chinese computer hacking attacks. The unit is, however, stationed in Pudong, Shanghai, not in the Underground Great Wall.

The existence and information about the Tuidang (Quit

the Party) movement in China, as described in the story, are, to the best of my knowledge, accurate.

My apologies to the management of the Le Bernardin restaurant in New York, the Venetian Resort Hotel and Casino in Macau, the Peninsula Hong Kong, and Gaddi's restaurant for running unauthorized fictitious spy operations on your premises.

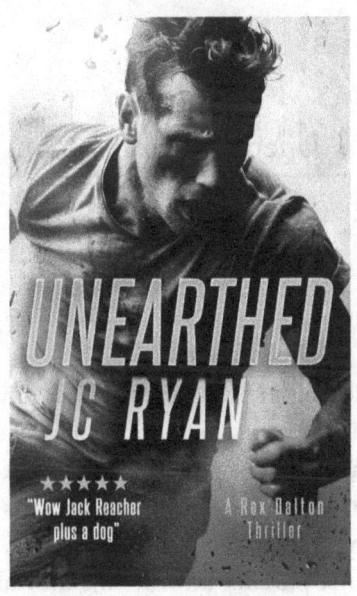

Unearthed: Prologue

The sun was setting after another perfect day on Eldorado, the Krige family farm in the Khomas Hochland Mountains west of Windhoek, the capital of Namibia. A tiny smile was playing on Thea Naudé's beautiful face as she hummed along with the tunes of *Jonathan Livingston Seagull*. Neil Diamond was her parents' favorite singer of all time.

Thea inherited her love of rocks from her dad, Erwin Krige. From her mother, Mieke, she got her stunning looks and creative talent. She had a four-year bachelor's degree in geology from Stellenbosch University in South Africa and a three-year diploma in jewelry design from the Ruth Prowse School of Art in Cape Town. She was twenty-five when she finished her studies and returned to Namibia in 2015. Like her parents, she couldn't live in a city; she settled on the family farm and started a lapidary business. In 2018, she married her college sweetheart, the young neighboring farmer Pieter Naudé, and they'd decided to live on Eldorado. Pieter was two years older than her. His parents and only sibling had died in a tragic motor accident two years before. After they got married, they turned Eldorado and Pieter's farm into one big game farm.

Part of Thea's gemstone operation was a small laboratory equipped with leading technology using scanning electron microscopy and X-ray techniques with which she could perform thousands of analyzes per minute.

The reason for the smile was the machines had confirmed that her dad's instincts and basic field tests were spot-on—as they always were—when he quoted a slightly adapted version of Mark Twain's immortal words in a mimicked Texas drawl, "There's silver in them thar hills."

It was a significant discovery. Not one that would crash the price of silver on the world market, but enough for a small mining operation to turn a nice profit for five to ten years. Her dad had four small mining operations, producing semi-precious gemstones, copper, African blue sodalite, and marble in various locations in the Namib Desert. It had made him a rich man and provided work for more than a hundred and twenty people. This silver mine would double that income.

But she knew all too well how often prospectors would look for one mineral and stumble across something totally different and more valuable. Or, as she was about to find out, more perilous.

She stopped humming, blinked a few times, and shook her head. "Impossible," she whispered. The smile was gone. She added a few more conditions to the report generator and ran the query again.

A few seconds later, she stared at the report. "It can't be. There's something wrong with the software. Or the scanner. This means I'll have to run all the tests again."

But before she did, she retrieved two bags of old samples from another site from the storeroom, conducted a few tests, and compared the results with the original reports generated six months ago. "A hundred percent match. Absolutely nothing wrong with the scanner or the software."

She went to the farmhouse, found her husband in front of the TV, and dragged him to the lab. On the way, Pieter told her their dogs, Tom and Jerry, probably knew more about geology than he did.

"I don't need another geologist. I need someone to check my sanity."

Pieter had a degree in agriculture; he knew about animals and plants, and biology, and genetics, and book-keeping, and such. Geology? Not so much. He listened carefully as she stepped him through the tests she had conducted and the results they produced. He found no fault in her logic or procedures. And the equipment was functioning correctly—she'd already proved that.

It was approaching ten p.m. when Pieter pronounced, "It's with great confidence that I can say, very much to my relief, you haven't lost your sanity."

"But Pieter, this goes against everything that I've ever learned about rare-earth elements."

"Why? Did you not expect to find any in the samples? I understand the name rare-earth is a misnomer; they're not really scarce. Or am I mistaken?"

"Yes, the rare in the name is because rare-earth elements, REEs, although ubiquitous, are extremely difficult and expensive to extract. I expected to see REEs in the samples because we often associate them with igneous rocks derived from carbonate-rich magmas, in other words, volcanic rocks like these. But this ... this ..."

"What?"

"There are seventeen rare-earth elements—some of them are available in quantities as common as chromium, nickel, tungsten, and lead. Even the scarcest of them, thulium and lutetium, are nearly two hundred times more common than gold. But we rarely find REEs in economically exploitable concentrations. China has a world monopoly and produces about ninety percent of all REEs on earth. Well ... up till now... it seems."

"What does *that* mean?"

"These samples contain all seventeen rare-earths and in concentrations of a magnitude I've never seen, read, heard, or even dreamed possible."

"So, why do you look like one who saw a ghost? Is this not exciting news?"

"Pieter, REEs are to the electronics industry what oil is to the automotive industry."

"And China would stop at nothing to protect their monopoly?"

"Exactly."

"We need to talk to your dad."

"Absolutely. I'll let him and Mom know we'll be over for breakfast."

Unearthed: Chapter One

TAKE ME TO NAMIBIA–MY SOUL NEEDS TO BREATHE

Erongo Mountains, near Karibib, Namibia

From Eldorado to the Krige campsite in the Erongo mountains was about a ninety-minute drive. Erwin and Mieke were having their first cup of coffee, savoring the sunrise, when Kaiser stood and looked down the two-tracked dirt road. The characteristic ridge of hair on his back, running in the opposite direction from the rest of his coat, stood on end.

Once known as the African Lion Hound, the pedigreed Rhodesian Ridgeback was more native to southern Africa than Erwin was. Kaiser could trace his forebears back to the hunting and guarding dogs of the Khoekhoen or Khoikhoi people, a.k.a. the Hottentots, the traditional nomadic pastoralist indigenous population roaming southwestern Africa for over two thousand years. Ridgebacks have even, dignified temperaments, devotion, and affection for their masters but are reserved with strangers.

Erwin's great-grandfather arrived in Namibia in 1885, a

year after the German chancellor Otto von Bismarck established Deutsch-Südwestafrika (German South West Africa) as the first German colony. Over the years, small numbers of Germans immigrated to 'the only German colony suitable for colonization by Europeans.' Among them were traders, diamond miners, colonial officials, and soldiers known in Germany as *Schutztruppe*. In 1885, Heinrich Krige, Erwin's great grandfather, arrived as one of a contingent of *Schutztruppe*.

Heinrich Krige served in the wars with the indigenous Nama and Herero tribes. His grandfather, Karsten Krige, took part in the First World War when Germany lost all its colonies. Namibia was placed under the administration of South Africa. During World War Two, as a preventative measure, the South African government interned both Erwin's father and grandfather to keep them from joining the Nazis.

During the *Grensoorlog* (Border War), Namibia's War of Independence (1966 to 1989), his father served in the Kommandos, a general term used for special police and military forces in German, Dutch, and Afrikaans speaking countries. Erwin served in the same war as an infantryman for two years after finishing school in 1974 as part of his compulsory military service.

"Don't worry, Kaiser," said Erwin, scratching the dog's back. "It's Thea and Pieter."

Erwin was a sixty-five-year-old tall, sinewy, suntanned man with silver-gray hair and a face reminiscent of his rugged surroundings. His easygoing manner concealed an inner strength.

Erwin was about ten years old when he met his first love —rocks. It hit him in the heart like Cupid's arrow as he watched his father slice a geode (hollow rock). The light fell on the cluster of six-sided purple crystals inside the hollow for the first time in five million years. Amethyst. The crystals which ancient Greeks and Egyptians believed helped the wearers to control evil thoughts, kept them sober, warded off guilty and fearful feelings, and protected them from witchcraft.

He was in love. He scoured the hills and mountains on Eldorado and further afield in search of more rocks. Before long, he had his own basic lapidary equipment and started cutting, polishing, and engraving gemstones. In his quest for more knowledge about rocks, he enrolled for a four-year bachelor's degree in geology at Stellenbosch University near Cape Town, South Africa, in 1977, after completing his military service.

When he graduated cum laude at the end of 1980, he had learned enough to know how little he knew. Not only about rocks, but also about life and the people with whom he shared the planet. That was his answer to one of his professors, who asked him about his plans for the future, hoping he could steer the brilliant student to enroll for a doctorate.

The elderly scholar had nodded thoughtfully. "That, Mr. Krige, is the beginning of wisdom."

That was also when he realized he possessed what the Germans call the wanderlust—the yearning for far-off places, the opposite of homesickness.

He sold part of his gem collection, packed his rucksack, and flew to Auckland, New Zealand. Those were the days when he could buy one US dollar with seventy-five South African cents.

For nearly seven years, in search of the meaning of life and that far-off place, he worked on dairy farms in New Zealand, sheep stations, fruit farms, and mines in Australia's

Outback. He taught English to Taiwanese, Chinese, and Japanese. He waited tables, worked on cattle, alpaca, fruit, and wheat farms across the USA, Canada, and Europe, and drove heavy trucks in Alaska. He worked in gold mines, coal mines, copper mines, and salt mines, and he traveled through South America, Europe, and the Middle East.

On September 1, 1987, the first day of spring in the southern hemisphere, he got another visit from the Roman god of love, Cupid, on Italy's Amalfi Coast. Her name was Mieke Opperman; she was almost as tall as he was. She had dark hair and deep brown eyes. She was more beautiful, colorful, and vibrant than any precious or semi-precious stone he had ever laid eyes on. Like him, she had been born and bred in Namibia. She was six years his junior, a nature photographer and painter on her OE (Overseas Experience) *au pairing* in Germany, France, and Italy to still *her* wanderlust. But above all, they were of a kindred spirit. Three months later, they were married.

And then, about a month after their wedding, while trying to make a new year's resolution on the first day of January 1988, a little over seven years after leaving Stellenbosch University, he discovered the far-off place he had been looking for. It was the country of his birth all along. He just had to see all the other places in the world to realize it.

"Take me to Namibia; my soul needs to breathe," he said to Mieke.

She had thrown her arms around his neck and whispered, "I thought you'd never ask."

Erwin's parents were still living on the farm when he and Mieke returned. Erwin loved the farm, but not farming. He and Mieke got a Mining Claims license, bought a Toyota Landcruiser and a caravan, and headed for the

Spitzkoppe in the Namib Desert, 150 kilometers east from Swakopmund.

The license is available only to Namibian citizens for small-scale mining. It is valid for an initial three-year period and multiple two-year extensions, provided the claim is being developed. They could hold a maximum of ten claims at a time.

Although Erwin grew up as a Christian, it was more out of tradition than belief. The deep-seated belief in God came on June 4, 1989. It happened in a single instant when he held the tiny, rumple-faced, dark-haired bundle of life in his callused hands for the first time. Tears were welling in his eyes when he said, "Let's call her Thea, the Greek word for a gift from God."

Erwin Krige often proclaimed himself to be one of the richest men on earth. His wealth had nothing to do with the number of digits in his bank balance, although that would definitely have placed him in the well-to-do bracket in any country. His wealth came from discovering the secret of eternal contentment—love of God, love of his wife and daughter, and doing what he loved in the country that he loved.

He found humanity's perpetual quest for proof of the existence of God amusing. "You'll find the answer in Namibia," he would've told them if they asked.

Grab your copy...
vinci-books.com/unearthed